I0642718

THE HOUSE OF GREY
VOLUME 1

THE HOUSE OF GREY
BOOK 1

COLLIN EARL

SILVERSTONE BOOKS

The House of Grey- Volume #1

By Collin Earl

Copyright 2025, SilverStone Books. All rights reserved.

This ebook is licensed for your personal enjoyment only. This ebook may not be re-sold or given away to other people. If you would like to share this book with another person, please purchase an additional copy for each recipient. If you're reading this book and did not purchase it, or it was not purchased for your use only, then please purchase your own copy. Thank you for respecting the hard work of this author.

ISBN-13: 978-1-967473-00-7

CONTENTS

PROLOGUE

IT WAS an average day in Western Washington, where average people went about their average lives. These average folks went to work and school, got stuck in traffic, and opened businesses for another day. School kids played in oversized raincoats while mud spattered around their ankles and large droplets of rain ran the length of their Scotch-guarded clothing. Parents moved slowly through water-covered streets as they navigated the early morning of one of the wettest days of the year.

Ironically enough, it is these average days that so often become more than just an average day. Why, might you ask, did this day that started like all the rest become more than average? Well, it started with the dream of a man and a boy, a whole lot of studying, and a little bit of luck.

An important-looking man stood on a stage in an event center in downtown Seattle. He was very well dressed, as if he were hosting a black-tie event. His brown hair was groomed to perfection, and the glare of stage lights reflected off his white teeth. He spoke to a huge crowd of people in a smooth, almost silky voice.

"Ladies and gentlemen, in my five years of hosting this competition, I have never seen anything like this. Our Challenger and Champion are neck and neck as they go into the final questions of the afternoon."

Cheers erupted all around as the huge crowd bellowed its approval at the man's words. This crowd was a spectacular one, composed of all kinds of people. Every age, sex, race, and ethnicity was present because, for the first time in fifteen years, the Coren University Academic Scholarship Competition had come down to its last round, to its last question. This was a great day for those who believed in and cheered for the underdog, as they believed this particular one had a real chance to upset. An upset that, for more than one secretive and unfair reason, should not be happening—should not happen now, or ever.

This underdog looked the part, but he was not playing his assigned role well at all. Although clearly from humble origins, he spoke eloquently, neither abashed nor intimidated, blending in well among an unfamiliar crowd. He was handsome, with thick hair of the darkest black, extraordinary blue-gray eyes, and a kind face. He gave off an air of both importance and conviction that was infectious. In truth, every time he stood to answer a question, a portion of the crowd would break into raucous applause. They wanted him to win, and they wanted him to feel that they wanted him to win . . . and feel it he did. The young man, being the humble sort, merely smiled in reaction to the crowd, showing his gratitude with the slightest of gestures. An occasional, almost embarrassed wave and a simple smile made the mothers and daughters sway and the fathers wonder what they needed to do to raise a young man like that.

This competition was an uphill battle for this young man, an unknown in all circles from the political to the popular. He swept onto the scene with blaring intelligence, decimating contestants more than three years his senior. Slowly, the hearts of those who witnessed his struggle melted as, over and over again, he fired off answers to history's mysteries. Things went so well that by the time the finals came around, the underdog was not so "under" anymore.

The man hosting the event put up a hand as the crowd, in the spirit of competition, let out another thunderous round of applause. He showed them a toothy smile.

"Now it has all come down to this, ladies and gentlemen, our challenger still holding strong right behind our champion as we go into the final round."

More applause and catcalls split the air.

"Let me remind our audience of the scoring scale. Each question is worth five points, with the ability to pass to their opponent up to three questions, in addition to a 'doubler' in each round. Depending on how quickly you answer, the doubler can become a ten-point question."

The crowd was not paying attention to this part. This was just a wannabe game show host doing his wannabe game show thing. They had heard all this explained before, but wait—

"I know what you are thinking," the man said, his coy smile becoming more mischievous by the second. "*We know all this. Why are you repeating it?* Well, ladies and gentlemen, I'll tell you why I'm repeating myself: This round is going to be a little different."

The crowd went silent at his words. Something different, they asked collectively. What could they possibly do differently? No, they couldn't change it now. Do **not** mess with the status quo; there is too much at stake.

"I would remind you," he said, gaining momentum now that he knew he had their attention, "that you will all find out as we go into this last round." He turned and looked at a large television camera. "I will let you know all this and more—right after this."

People groaned at his pronouncement. It was given that an entertainer would cut to a commercial right when the show was getting exciting. For those in the audience, however, it was downright annoying.

Despite the relatively short break, most of the people in the audience grumbled as the stagehands made the necessary changes for the final round of the competition. Each person in the audience took little notice of those around them. Many, after all, were rich and important. Of course, with the success of this no-name challenger, the commoners seemed to come out of the woodwork. Well, the rich and important did not have time for mingling with commoners. Keep your distance—it was an unspoken rule. However, every rule has an exception, and this one was no different.

A young girl, no older than five, sat in the back row in the last seat of the hall. She was beautifully dressed—with perfectly arranged hair courtesy of her personal stylist. Her family typically spent the day shopping at the most expensive stores, eating at the very best restaurants, and whiling away the hours on the streets of Seattle. Now they sat in a stuffy hall watching some sort of game show. In truth, she was too far back to really see what was happening and a little too young to even appreciate it. To her credit, she tried to act interested; she really did. Mommy and Daddy were acting like this was important, but she just couldn't get her heart into it, no matter how hard she tried.

What was the big deal anyway? There were so many people here, and they were all paying close attention, especially to the pretty boy at the front. Actually, she wasn't even sure he was a boy. He kind of looked like a girl. There was a noise behind the girl, startling her. She turned her little frame to peer over her shoulder. There was a man. She blinked in confusion. Was he there before? She thought back to when she entered the hall. She didn't remember anyone being there, but she hadn't been paying close attention. She pondered a moment more. No, he couldn't have been there before. She was in the last row in the last seat. He must have moved his chair to that corner, but she would have heard him; she would have noticed. Wouldn't she?

The girl pivoted again in her seat to look at him, trying to move so he wouldn't notice. He was a funny man, wasn't he? He sat completely stationary, not moving at all. She wondered why he wasn't moving. Maybe he was sleeping? This seemed like an odd place to sleep. She put his lack of movement aside for a moment as she noticed something else.

You really are a funny man, aren't you? Why are you wearing such a big overcoat and hood? She laughed. His coat was funny, too. It didn't have any place for the arms. She giggled a bit more. Isn't that weird? Why make a coat without armholes? Oh, wait. Maybe he was one of those people she saw on the road from time to time, the ones with the signs. A sad feeling crept into her heart. He had a funny coat because he couldn't afford another one. And . . . and she had laughed at him. How mean! That's not something you should do. She had to apologize. That's what you do, right? When you make a mistake, you say I'm sorry. But it looked like he was still sleeping. Should she wake him? If she did, she would have to apologize for waking him, too! What should she do?

Oddly enough, as if he had been listening to her thoughts, the man sat up, one eye visible under the hood of the coat. It was a minute or so before she noticed.

She gave a start as she saw the dark eye of the man. Could eyes really even be that dark? It looked almost black. The girl continued to feel confused. Why did he pick black when something like pink is so much nicer? Grownups sure did funny things sometimes.

She knew better than to talk to strangers, but her childish curiosity got the better of her; she lifted up a hand and waved.

The man smiled back.

Oh, what a nice smile. You should really smile more often; you wouldn't be so scary. Hey, what are you doing?

The man sat up a little straighter and leaned toward the little girl. Despite the fact that she had decided he was a nice man, she shrank back. OK, he was still a little scary.

The man lifted a hand out from underneath his funny coat, showing her there was nothing in it.

Oh, I see, you are about to do magic, aren't you? There was something like this at her birthday party last year. This man, however, was a bit different than the clown she had seen so many months ago. When the clown did magic, he showed her and her friends his hands. At first, nothing was in them; then, *poof*, there were flowers! It was amazing. Her brother had said it wasn't real, that the flowers were fake and had just been hidden. She, however, knew that was crazy. Flowers don't just appear, and magic really existed—she had seen it. The little girl wondered if this man really was going to do magic.

She was not disappointed.

He was performing magic, though his way was much different than the clown's. She thought that he was praying or something as he did some weird movement with his first two fingers while they pointed in the air.

Many questions bobbled around her head as she tried her best to comprehend what the man was doing. She received another shock as a funny light gathered around the man's hand. Was she seeing this right?

This new light didn't last long, as suddenly, a lollipop appeared! The little girl's eyes brightened as she looked at the lollipop. It was multicolored and as big as her head. Maybe he would share.

Oh, that's not how you hold a lollipop! You're going to drop it.

The man had taken the sucker and placed it stick down on the palm of his hand. He was balancing it on the palm of his hand. It sat there completely still. Frozen.

She looked on in awe, transfixed at the sight before her. This was unfortunate because if she had been less distracted by the lollipop, she would have noticed his rather suspicious behavior.

"Welcome back, ladies and gentlemen!" rang out the voice of the man on stage, effectively catching the attention of all those in the audience. "Now, allow me to explain our exciting change of…"

The girl stopped listening again. She didn't understand what the silly man at the front was talking about anyway. Besides, the man with the lollipop was much more—Hey, where did it go?

The lollipop was gone! He'd eaten it all? No way! He didn't even share! And she had thought he was a nice man. The girl sat back in her seat, feeling sad. Suddenly, there was a tap on her shoulder.

It was the man, and he was giving her a weird look. He was awfully hard to understand, this man with the funny coat. His two fingers were up again and moving quickly through the air, much faster than they had before. Are you praying again? But then why did you tap me on the shoulder?

Out of nowhere, he spoke.

"Look in your pocket."

His voice was soft, almost musical. It had an indefinable effect on the girl. She felt lighter, though she didn't understand why. She did what she was told. Slowly, she reached her hand into her pocket.

She felt something. What did she feel? It was small, long, round, and hard. What . . . what could it be?

She started to pull at the object in her pocket when the lollipop came out with a small jerk. No, wait, that's impossible. It's too big. There is no way! Should . . . ?

A voice interrupted her.

"Well, it's about time to go to work."

The man. He had spoken. Softly, yet with brilliance. Almost forgetting the sucker in her hand, the girl once again turned.

He was praying again.

Two fingers pointed upward and again moved with curious gestures. Up, down, left, right, half circle. They were too fast. She couldn't keep track.

More light? It was coming from his sleeve again. What was happening?

The young girl jumped as the crowd let out a collective moan. The loud man at the front was talking fast. The girl turned back toward the stage in time to see the pretty boy standing with an arm raised in triumph. He appeared to be scanning the back of the hall, looking, searching.

Before the girl could figure out what was going on, she was distracted again, this time by the loud man with the microphone.

"I don't believe it!" he almost screamed, "I don't believe it! For the first time in the history of Coren University, a FRESHMAN has won!"

What? It's over? And the boy who looks like a girl won? Wait, isn't this all pretend? He wasn't supposed to win. Mommy and Daddy had said the winner had already been decided.

She heard a small snicker.

The man. The man behind her. The boy, the boy up front. He had been searching. Who had he been searching for? The girl turned back around to the man.

Only there was nothing there. No man, no funny coat, not even a chair. But she still had the lollipop. He had been there.

"Are you enjoying your sucker, honey?" asked the girl's mother in a sweet voice. "Try to save some for later. We're going to eat soon."

What? How did she know about the lollipop? She hadn't shown Mommy, Daddy, or anyone.

"Remember, if you're a good girl, we'll go back to the Fun Factory and get you another sometime."

"Mommy," the girl replied, unsure of herself. She noticed a funny, almost glazed look in her mother's eyes, like she was dreaming. "What do you mean?"

"Silly girl," her mother answered, "you must be tired. Had a bit too much excitement for one day? Your father bought that sucker this afternoon at the Fun Factory, remember? It's your favorite candy store."

"Oh," the girl said. "But Mommy, I didn't—"

The girl cut herself short. Her mother was no longer paying attention, and the dreamy look was gone from her eyes. Her brother had just walked up to their row from the stage, and he looked disappointed.

Fun Factory? She didn't go to the Fun Factory today, did she? There was a man. He had a funny coat. He gave her a lollipop. He had been here. The girl turned again, looking for the man she now wasn't sure existed.

CHAPTER 1
A NEW PLACE

AN OLDER-LOOKING minivan rode smoothly up Main Street in a town in Western Washington. A young man slept under a blanket in the back while a chubby yet cute middle-aged woman with mocha brown hair drove, whistling tunelessly.

"Monson, honey, we're here."

Monson Grey awoke with a start but immediately closed his eyes again. He had been sleeping, and Molly totally woke him up. Uncool. Completely and totally uncool.

"Molly, not only was I actually sleeping, I was having the best dream ever! Curse you, you irritatingly spiteful woman, for waking me up."

"Oh, stop your whining. We're here." Molly pointed at a huge granite sign with the words *Coren University* written upon it. "This is a momentous occasion. This is the time when—"

Monson interrupted. "When you finally realize how stupid an idea this is?"

"The Monson Grey wit strikes again. I remember you being more pleasant before the incident."

"I remember you being nicer."

"Har har har, you're hilarious. You don't remember anything. I could be the mistress of the devil himself, and you wouldn't know any better."

"Well, the joke's on you, Molly. I'm already well aware of your tempestuous affair with the prince of darkness, but what does that have to do with anything? I'm also well informed about my memory loss, thanks. I'm the one who woke up in the hospital not knowing who I was, remember?"

She rolled her eyes. "How could I forget? You use it as an excuse every two seconds."

Monson smiled sweetly. "Which brings me back to my point: Why do I have to go to this school again?"

Molly threw her wallet at him. "He wanted you at this school, and it's completely paid for, so stop complaining."

Monson put his head under the blanket. "Can't wait."

Molly turned the car up University Street, and Monson finally got his first real eyeful of the school that was to become his home.

Coren University had an elite, Ivy League feel to it—an ideal the grounds and buildings took to extremes. The campus sprawled wastefully, taking up the better part of the valley, which was nestled in the middle of the only temperate rain forest in the world. No expense was spared on this school for rich kids, and Monson was already tired of the place.

A brick wall several dozen feet high encased much of the grounds. The wall was layered with vines so dense that the brick was barely visible. There would be no climbing those bad boys.

Monson's annoyance grew. It was bad enough that the mountains surrounding the city of Coren permitted only one way in or out, but now he felt like he was entering not a school but a fortress, or worse yet, a prison. Looking at the wall, Monson half-expected to see battlements with crossbow-carrying sentries overlooking the incoming class. He didn't, of course, but he did see cameras.

Surveillance. Great.

Monson half-grinned as he thought about crossbows. Now that would be cool.

He continued to scan the vines looking for... well, he didn't know exactly what he was looking for. Possible escape routes? Was it odd to scout the area for escape routes? Maybe. But who was going to call him out on it? He didn't know anyone. Besides, it was a habit of his, so he was grateful. Memory loss tended to make you grateful for odd things.

Once Monson and Molly entered the campus, the road forked, one branch continuing to run parallel to the large brick wall and the other curving out of view into the woods. After a few more minutes of driving, they reached an enormous iron gate where the road veered off in a circle, doubling back on itself. Molly pulled in behind a black Cadillac Escalade and stopped the car. Her hands were shaking in anticipation.

She grabbed her purse. "Now where did I put that blasted key card?"

"Key card?" asked Monson.

"Yes—key card. Everything here is coded."

"Coded?"

"We aren't going to get a lot done if you repeat everything I say," Molly teased. "Yes, coded. You're going to need your card for everything here."

"That sucks." Monson could already sense the restrictions implied by that little tidbit. "Why would they do that?"

As Molly started to reply, the Escalade darted forward.

"We're up!" She pulled into the now-vacant space, rolled down the window, and scooted up as close as she could to a large display screen.

"Welcome to Coren University," said a slightly robotic voice. "Insert key card identification, please."

Molly pulled out a small white envelope, opened it, and retrieved a blue key card. She placed the card in the computer display slot. As Monson watched Molly, a rare feeling of affection welled up in him. You couldn't help but love someone like Molly. She was fun, and though she didn't act like it, smart. Molly's presence in this particular venture was extra fortunate, as she happened to be considerably more excited about Coren than he was. He did not want to be here—she was making him. But she was the adult; he was the kid. What could he do?

Big bold letters appeared on the screen at the same time the computer said, "Mr. Grey, *Horum Vir*. Welcome to Coren University—"

"What the hell did it just say?" Monson asked, drowning out the rest of the computer's greeting and raising an eyebrow.

"Don't swear, dear," Molly said, trying to listen to the rest of the message. Finally convinced that there wasn't any more to be heard, she started to pull forward, saying, "I think we go this way."

"You didn't answer my question," Monson said, looking around as they entered the parking lot.

"I know." She glanced around, presumably looking for a parking spot.

Monson gritted his teeth. He HATED it when she did that. She had a really annoying habit of ignoring whatever she deemed unimportant.

Parking was a nightmare, due mostly to the considerable number of students, parents, and attendants. There seemed to be as many servants as students in this place; probably something to be expected at a school like Coren. The student population was exceptionally diverse, which Monson liked, but there was a noticeable socioeconomic gap; that he had not expected. Considering Coren was the wealthiest and most exclusive private school in the world, many of the students played their part and arrived in style. Stretch limousines in every make and color littered the visitor's parking lot, each arrival trying to outdo the last. Other expensive modes of transportation were also plentiful, including helicopters, jets, and to Monson's delight, a hovercraft. Now *that* wasn't something one saw every day.

Monson was relieved to see many people like himself. These were not the ultra-rich, but regular, clean-cut folks with normal-looking families and friends coming to see them off as they started on a path toward a hopeful future. This was a good school, after all, so they should be hopeful. Monson looked again. Hmm . . . there were more scholarship students than he'd expected. That made him happy, somehow.

Monson observed the variety of students and families, curious how the different social classes would interact. At least that was his intention; the large number of good-looking girls in the crowd made it difficult. After a while, he gave up entirely and looked at the ground.

Monson wondered what it was going to be like being around this many people—this many *girls*. This was going to be the biggest challenge yet, he just knew it, and he *so* did not feel up to it. Nurses, even hot ones, in a hospital for weeks on end were one thing. Girls his own age were quite another. Right on cue, Molly pointed across the parking lot.

"Oh, Monson, honey, look at her."

Monson gasped.

"Molly!" He tried to grab her hand. "Don't point! I have to go to school with these people!"

"Fine," she said, "but look anyway."

Monson turned to where Molly pointed. A girl was talking animatedly with a large group of people.

Molly was right; she is pretty smokin', Monson thought to himself. Her waves of long golden hair were pulled back into a deliberately messy half-ponytail; a pleasing contrast to her perfectly proportioned face. She was strikingly gorgeous. Her fashionable dress boasted social conservatism and attested to the fact that not only did she have money, but she occupied a place in high society. Her hands never seemed to be out of place. She smiled at exactly the right moments. She moved and gestured with poise and refinement. She was a proper lady.

Monson looked her up and down a second time and half-smiled. Despite the lady's forceful appeal to modest precepts, and though the simplicity of her dark silken skirt and pure white blouse left much to the imagination, the flow of the material as it enveloped a soft and curvy figure caught the attention of more than one boy in the parking lot. She would have been even prettier if a nasty sneer wasn't etched onto her features.

"She's a cute one," Molly said as they pulled into a parking space on the far side of the lot.

"Is that a question or a statement?" Monson asked, pulling open the door as the car rolled to a stop. "Never mind, it doesn't have anything to do with me."

"You stop that right now. I am expecting you to be social at this school," she said, smiling encouragingly. "They're going to love you. I mean, how could they not?"

"Yeah, I wonder!" Monson said sarcastically. "How could they not love *me*? I'm so freaking lovable."

"I'm sensing some sarcasm," Molly said, her eyes narrowing slightly.

"I hope so. I'm laying it on pretty thick."

She glared at him, though it wasn't convincing; she was trying not to laugh.

"Anyway, I'll be right back. Start unloading the car while I go check on something." She strolled toward a building in the center of the parking lot.

Grumbling, Monson put his effort into getting the gate of the minivan open but stopped when he noticed his reflection. He was quite the sight.

Long, dark, wavy hair hid a once-handsome countenance. Scars, many of them, stretched across his face, vying for dominance with his soft gray eyes, straight nose, and strong jawline. A flicker of movement in the reflection caught his eye. Monson pushed his hair out of his eyes and peered closer. He didn't see anything but his obvious need for a haircut. His appearance scared most that made his acquaintance, so he let his hair grow, hoping that it might help to hide his scars. He wasn't sure this worked; the hair may have just exacerbated the problem. He had experience with such. One night while still in the hospital, he scared a new nurse out of her skin when he came up behind her in the middle of the night. The woman's right hook narrowly missed the side of his jaw. He actually had to pin her against the wall before she would listen to him.

"You aren't going to hurt me, are you?" He could still remember how her voice quivered with fear.

"Hurt you?" his reply came back. "You were the one who tried to hit me."

After a few minutes of explanation, he let go of her. She stared at him.

"I'm sorry," her voice came. The fear was still prevalent. "I didn't realize who you were."

"Yeah, I get that a lot."

"You're the one, aren't you?" Her tone changed. "You're the one from Baroty Bridge."

"Yeah, that's the rumor, isn't it?"

"What's your name?"

He walked away from her. She called after him.

"Wait," she pleaded. "Don't go, I didn't . . . mean to offend—"

"You didn't offend me."

"Then why—"

He turned back to look at her. "I can't tell you what I don't remember."

He never saw that nurse again.

It was not a pleasant exchange, but that experience taught him a valuable lesson. His past life, what he knew of it, was gone. Things were different now. While he had been forced to learn a life lesson, an important one, it was one that was better learned sooner rather than later.

He remembered his name now, but in many ways he was like a clean slate with bits of himself reappearing on occasion. There was much he could not remember about his life. Pieces of himself still felt lost, and yet he did not suffer from depression like many would expect. He didn't know any different; he didn't know what it was like to be treated kindly by strangers, so he didn't bother worrying about it. Now, he worked with the situation that life presented to him, careful to notice if he was making anyone uncomfortable, but never backing down because of his appearance.

Monson noticed a group of students passing his van. They looked older, probably upperclassmen. Their gazes shifted over him as if he was part of the landscape, until one of them, a portly girl with frumpy brown hair, stopped to mentally register what she was looking at. She grabbed her nearest companion and spun her toward Monson. They looked like they were going to be sick.

Monson ignored them and switched his attention back to the van's gate as he moved mindlessly; his focus was not really on what he was doing. His thoughts strayed to the blonde girl. She really was a beauty. He might not be able to talk to her, but he could watch. That was more than he was able to do in the hospital, and that was something.

Monson smiled, pulled out his bags, and stacked them. He wondered idly what his teachers were like and what kind of friends he would make, assuming of course that he made any at all. Monson never had many friends out in the country. Well, maybe he had lots of friends, but he couldn't remember them. No one had visited him in the hospital, so he assumed that he didn't. It was kind of a depressing thought.

After ten minutes or so, Monson was able to get his luggage and various belongings from the different locations inside the van. It was absolutely amazing how much stuff could scatter within the limited space.

Monson did a quick scan, only to see a long cloth pouch that until then had failed to catch his attention. Monson grabbed it and was surprised. Whatever was inside was hard, heavy, and from what he could feel through the plush covering, curiously smooth. A familiar ache tingled in Monson's fingers. Excited, he pulled open the pouch and removed a highly polished stick.

This was not what Monson had expected.

The wood was smooth and extremely dense, which led Monson to believe it was probably made of some sort of tough wood, like cherry or oak. At first, Monson thought it was a cane or some forgotten decoration, but a slight curve in the construction put that theory to rest.

Monson brought the stick to eye level.

Around three and a half feet long and two inches in diameter, the stick had a handle that was a fraction thicker than the rest of it. It ran straight up for a few inches where it met the blade, then the whole thing curved back slightly as it reached its tip. The wood was dark and a lot heavier than it looked. Monson took the stick in a double-fisted grip and swung it.

Strange. This funny stick was . . . was like . . . a sword or something. Thoughts, images, and sensations swept through him: the touch of steel, the strain of aching muscles, and the feeling of the elements— fire, wind, water, and earth. The sensations vanished as quickly as they arrived, while Monson stared at the wooden sword.

Fascinating, Monson thought. Now what on earth are you doing here?

Monson tensed as a sensation prickled his neck. Straining his ears, his only warning was a *whoosh* before he heard footsteps directly behind him. He reacted instinctively, raising the polished stick and flinging it over his shoulder, almost like a knight grabbing for a shoulder-slung sword. There was a smack as the wood made contact with some unknown object. Monson's body again reacted as he arched his back slightly, slid with a fluid grace, and spun to face his attacker.

There was a boy standing in front of him holding a stick similar to the one in Monson's hand. He held it in a neutral position with a thoroughly shocked look on his face. Monson gave him an appraising look and thought, with a sense of shock that mirrored the boy's, that this person couldn't be a student; he could hardly be considered an adolescent. He was too big, too well-muscled, and had too much facial hair. They continued to gape at each other, neither of them moving or saying a word.

The stranger was a rugged fellow, tall and muscular with short, reddish-blond hair, light green eyes, and well-kept stubble. He wore nice clothing: a blue button-up with tan linen slacks pressed to perfection, accessorized with a white gold Rolex. A highly polished stick, much like Monson's, dropped to his side as he stared with a dimwitted expression.

"Wait a minute, you aren't Casey! Sorry about that—I thought you were someone else."

Monson couldn't help it. He laughed. The boy looked slightly embarrassed and on the verge of apologizing again. Monson spoke before he could.

"I would hate to see what you do to people you actually know," Monson said, gesturing to the stick in the boy's hand. "What would have happened if I hadn't blocked it?"

"I think it's probably better that we don't think about it," the boy said.

The boy's eyes, which appeared slightly cloudy, went a little wide, like he was coming out of some sort of trance. Monson knew that he was looking at his messed-up face and just now noticing with whom he was talking.

"You look like you got in a fight with a meat grinder and lost."

Monson laughed again. *That* was unexpected.

"At least I have an excuse," Monson shot back, "which is more than I can say for you."

"What's that supposed to mean?"

Monson's answer was lost to a loud voice that echoed behind the larger boy.

"EN GARDE!"

"What in the—" Monson moved in a jerky and abrupt fashion. He hadn't sensed this one; he was caught totally off-guard. Monson reacted quickly, ducking and rolling to his side out of harm's way. He looked up in time to see a second boy quickly traverse the distance between them.

Luckily for Monson, the new boy had apparently found his target: the larger redheaded boy. Wood cracked as the boys threw their weight into their respective attacks. A flurry of movement coupled with laughter resounded as the onslaught commenced.

The first boy, the redhead, was fending off some rapid blows from the much smaller newcomer. What this new boy lacked in size he made up for in pure speed and spirit. Moving from pose to pose with rapid succession, his style, which seemed to change from time to time, was wild but powerful and extraordinarily effective. The larger boy fought valiantly but was slowly overpowered. Monson found the contest before him exciting, which caused him to look down at the stick in his hand.

Have I done this before?

A whistle from the direction of the fight interrupted his reverie. The large boy, still fending off attacks, whistled and then gestured toward Monson's right hand. Monson knew immediately what he was asking for and took aim, flicking his stick toward the scuffle.

Exhibiting some fine agility, the redhead caught the stick. New life entered him as he renewed his offense and took his attacker by surprise. With a great deal of finesse, he started to counterattack with a double-handed fencing style, spinning and slicing through the air like a human food processor.

Notwithstanding, Monson could tell the conclusion was pretty much inevitable; the smaller attacker was just too fast for his larger opponent. The duel concluded in a dramatic disarmament by the newcomer. With a few parries and thrusts, Monson saw the redhead's sticks fly far overhead and hit the ground with a loud clang.

"Got you, Arthur," the new boy said, landing the tip of the stick on the former's throat. "That's one for me. It appears you're in for a bad year."

"Don't get cocky, Casey!" Arthur shot back angrily. "First day of school *and* you were lucky. You caught me off-guard."

The new boy laughed. Turning around, he looked toward Monson.

Dressed in expensive denim and a polo shirt, he was handsome, but for some reason, the style didn't suit him.

His features were normal enough, with dirty blond hair, a soft jawline, and smooth eyebrows. Yes, he was quite normal except for the eyes: They seemed a bit large for his face, almost like his mom had mated with a bat. Monson could tell that the boy came from money, just like the cute blonde girl, but the effect of the expensive clothes was lost in the sweaty figure standing before him. Another unexpected detail: The boy's hands were rough and callused, worn and heavy with use. Monson was impressed. This boy knew a hard day's work. Monson watched as he lobbed his mock sword from hand to hand. It looked very much at home.

"Who's the new guy?" asked the boy called Casey, gesturing toward Monson. He stared at Monson, narrowing his eyes. "And what happened to his face?"

Monson breathed deeply. It was about time to make his exit.

"No idea," Arthur said, also looking at Monson. "I actually attacked him thinking it was you."

"You attacked him thinking it was me? HA! How thick are you?"

"Shut up, Casey."

"Better watch it, Arthur," Casey said, swinging the stick back in an arc and flourishing it outrageously. "I don't want to have to give you another thrashing."

"Oh, is that what it was?" asked Arthur, who sounded like he was starting to get angry. "How about I pull out the surburito and crush that fat melon of yours right now?"

"Bring it on!" Casey said, also sounding riled up. "I'll stomp the fool out of you."

"Guys, calm down," Monson said rashly, moving to stand between them. "We still have orientation to attend, and let's face it, it's way too early in the morning for a thrashing."

Surprise etched in their sweaty faces, the two boys looked at each other and burst into laughter. Monson smiled at them, not quite sure what to do. He opened his mouth to say something, but realized that he couldn't think of anything, and shut it again. They all stood for a brief span more, Monson feeling awkward.

Getting his fill, Monson turned away, embarrassed. He walked away, preparing to grab his stuff and go hide in a hole, but before he could move more than a few feet, a hand found his shoulder and whipped him back around.

"Where do you think you're going?" Casey said, inspecting Monson with a beady eye.

"Well . . . I was just . . . ." Monson replied sheepishly. The two boys just smiled as they stood in silence.

"This is the part where you tell us your name," Casey whispered, extending the hand he had used to grab Monson. He didn't sound angry, quite the opposite in fact. Monson replayed the events quickly in his head. He was starting to feel kind of stupid.

"Monson," he said, shaking the outstretched hand, "Monson Grey. And you are?"

"Cassius Kay, but you can call me Casey. Everyone does." Casey gestured to the larger boy, who wasn't paying attention to the exchange of pleasantries but rather gazing at a group of girls several cars down. He had a comical look on his face as he eyed one of the girls longingly.

"The brute ogling the ladies is Arthur Paine. He—" But Casey was cut short when Arthur spun on his heel and bellowed angrily.

"How many times do I have to ask you not to call me Arthur?"

"I told you there's no way I'm calling you that ridiculous name," Casey said calmly. "I can't say it without laughing! That's how dumb a name it is!"

"It's based on Lucius Artorius Castus," Arthur said, a smug look on his face, "as in King Arthur. How could that ever be a dumb name?"

Casey moaned, covering his eyes with his hand. "How many times are we going to have to have this discussion? Artorius Castus doesn't exist, just as King Arthur doesn't exist. They weren't the same person because neither of them were real people. Besides, why would you change it to Artorius? Even if he were real, it's still a stupid name."

"And I've already told you, *Cassius*," Artorius said, trying to make Casey's name sound like an insult, "if Artorius wasn't real, then where did they get the Round Table, huh?"

He said it with *total* conviction.

"Did you really just ask me that?" Casey retorted.

"I hate to interrupt," Monson said before they got back into the swing of their argument, "but why *Artorius*? What's wrong with Arthur? I think it's a nice name. Why change it?"

Artorius sighed so deeply and with such melancholy that Monson had to wonder if he was serious. Artorius continued to look regretful, then said, "Do you know how many times I've been called Weasley in my lifetime?"

Monson looked at Casey, a smile on his face, his lips parted. Casey, however, preempted him.

"If you mention that book, I swear I'm going to punch you."

"Wouldn't dream of it, though have *you* considered changing your name to Dudley? I think it suits you."

"Oh, you are *so* going to get it!"

Monson laughed, but Casey wasn't done yet.

"Ok, back to my original question. What happened to your face?"

"Casey!" Artorius stammered, "You can't say things like that!"

"What are you talking about?" Monson interjected. "You asked if I got in a fight with a meat grinder! How is that any better?"

Artorius looked confused. "Is that bad? I thought it was rather manly."

Casey sneered. "Only you would think that was manly."

Casey looked back to Monson, obviously wanting him to answer. Monson smiled. He liked these two already.

"Don't be jealous of my dashing good looks."

"Don't worry about that."

Monson, the retort on the tip of his tongue, was cut short by a call he recognized as Molly's. He totally forgot; they had somewhere to be. Gathering himself, he turned back toward the boys and said, "We'd better get moving. We don't want them to start without us."

"Hold on," Casey said, starting to move away. "I'll get my crap and meet you guys at the central passage. You'd better go too, *Arthur*. I expect your mommy is waiting for you."

"Bite me," Arthur growled, hurrying away. Casey laughed and cantered out of sight. Monson collected his belongings, including the mock weapon that lay forgotten on the ground. Once situated, he started to move purposefully toward Molly, who was standing not far away, beckoning Monson toward her.

"Are you ready?" she asked as he neared her. She was eyeing him expectantly. He nodded but didn't say anything. Molly grabbed one of his bags and started toward the far corner of the parking lot. They walked briskly, chatting amicably. Monson wasn't really that interested; he was still thinking about the two boys he had just met. Eventually, they fell in behind a large group of parents and students who were talking quietly about something. There was a hint of conspiracy in their voices.

"He's here? What do you mean, he's here?" a tall blonde woman was asking a man who appeared to be her husband. "Isn't he supposed to be locked up somewhere? I heard he's a criminal."

"Those are all rumors. Actually, from what I heard, they don't really know where he's been. Just that he disappeared suddenly and now is back. They weren't even sure he was going to redeem the position," the man said, leaning into his wife. "To think the new *Horum Vir* is someone like that when the Diamond is still attending. Preposterous."

Diamond? As in the stone? Monson thought as a feeling of déjà vu assaulted him. He thought back to their entrance into the guest parking lot and the computerized voice. His curiosity sparked, Monson turned to Molly and whispered, "What's a *Horum Vir*? It sounds familiar."

Molly smiled and patted him on the shoulder. "Not a *what*,

Monson," she said, "but a *who.*" Monson, confused, looked at Molly, his gaze unwavering, waiting for her to explain. When she didn't say anything, he said, "Molly, do you know something that you aren't telling me?"

"Monson, honey," Molly said vaguely, "this isn't the time. You know that I can't walk and talk at the same time. I get all tongue-twisted."

"Molly, we're standing still."

"How about that!"

"Molly Allison Pennmentail, cough it up!"

"Monson, dear," she said, her tone suddenly switching from happy to resigned, even weary, "there is something, but I don't know if you're quite ready. Now is just not the time."

He glared at her, trying to show his discontent. She didn't falter under his gaze but stood firmly, holding eye contact. It appeared that she was trying to hold back a smile.

"You're making fun of me." Monson's eyes narrowed. "Please tell me, what's the deal?"

"Oh, all right," she said, choking back a laugh. "You have to promise not to get mad. It's not like I wanted to hide anything from you; I was just—"

Artorius and Casey nudged into them, and Molly stopped talking. "Hey hey," Casey said, pulling in behind Monson. "Monson, honey, who are your friends?"

"Uh . . . uh," Monson stammered, trying to figure out how to explain that they weren't really his friends, but the big kid had attacked him thinking he was the short, wiry one. Casey, saving him an explanation, bowed and said, "I am called Casey. 'Tis a pleasure to meet such a fine and desirable lady."

"Dude," Artorius said, shoving Casey slightly, "what the heck are you bowing for? Nobody does that."

Casey glared at him, and then cracked a smile when he and Artorius made eye contact. Artorius glared back but also ended up grinning. He then took the opportunity to make his introduction.

"Artorius," he said, holding out a hand. "It's a pleasure to meet you."

Molly eyed them both for a second.

"Molly Pennmentail," she replied primly, ignoring his hand. Then, without warning, she bowed. Casey broke into a fit of laughter, and Artorius turned a bright red.

Molly and Monson joined in the laughter, as did Artorius . . . eventually.

Guided by lighted arrows, the students and parents migrated from the parking area into ornate covered walkways. As they moved along, Monson saw different groups of older students greet each other in a variety of ways from high fives to kisses, each of the students seeming to address each other in some unique way. Girls grouped together as if magnetically drawn to one another. The females laughed and whispered, eyeing boys expectantly, an air of secrecy lingering around them. Large groups of boys gathered in well-established and obvious cliques, with the normal clichéd partitions of jocks, geeks, and nerds doing their utmost to avoid one another. Monson gawked. There were a lot more people than he had expected. The realization made him uncomfortable.

The hallway divided into two paths that presumably led off into different parts of the school. Many of the older students followed the right fork of the hall while the rest, including Monson's group, steered to the left. Monson wondered where the others were going but didn't care enough to inquire. Casey was talking sports with Artorius and Molly. They seemed to be disagreeing over something.

"You're senile!" Artorius said bitterly. "I don't care how good we are, there is no way."

"Arthur, you have to have faith, brother," Casey said, slapping him on the back. "Once they see us play, they won't be able to keep us off the field."

"Casey," Artorius said in a reasonable tone, "all joking aside, you have to be realistic." He looked grim, like what he was saying was costing him a lot of effort. "There is no way that you and I are going to get on the top team, never mind actually playing. They have never had a freshman play varsity at Coren University. *Never*."

"You know," Molly said, smiling and placing a hand on Monson, "Monson is automatically on the team."

"What?!" Monson shot back, "What exactly am I automatically on?"

"The Legion," Molly said, acting as if this was the most obvious answer.

"Thanks, Molly," Monson replied sarcastically, "and what is the Legion?"

Casey was the one who answered. "The Coren University football team," he said in awe.

"How did you do that?" Artorius asked, looking slightly annoyed.

"I have no idea," Monson said with mild shock. He looked inquiringly at Molly. She merely smiled but said nothing. Casey and Artorius were both looking at Monson with something close to reverence. Monson felt his face turning red. He quickly started examining the courtyard and buildings that were now in front of them in order to avoid the gazes of Casey and Artorius.

"OK, Grey," Casey said, breaking the silence. "I gotta ask, how did you pull—"

He was cut off when Molly placed a hand on his shoulder.

Apparently, she didn't want him asking any questions.

The courtyard of Coren University looked like it belonged in a brochure for ancient Rome. The yard was completely enclosed by a small rock wall about three feet tall and a walkway that ran parallel to it. The path zigzagged between large oaks and willows and was accented by lush and well-kept lawns. An abundance of gardens with all kinds of flowers and shrubs, many of which were on the tail end of blooming, added just the right touch of the outdoors. The gardens were perfect . . . or close to it.

On the opposite side of the gardens, in the distance, older students pushed toward a large, looming building that was extravagantly lit.

His group of what Monson could only assume was new students continued down the largest of the rocky paths looking nervous but excited. They walked for what seemed like a long time, owing partly to the sheer size of the campus. The nervous atmosphere probably caused that feeling to intensify, making the walk feel longer than it really was. As they traveled farther along, the students saw many buildings scattered around the grounds. Monson noticed the names of each building on large stone slabs placed methodically in front. The plaques were inscribed with names like "Caesar's Hall" and "Home of the Five Good Emperors." Casey and Artorius seemed to be enjoying the grandeur of Coren University just as much as he was. In the short time he had known the two boys, this was the quietest they had been.

The three boys and Molly followed the other new students, who collectively seemed to know where they were going, until they came to the doors of a massive building. The slab outside it said 'Coliseum'. It resembled a mix between modern architecture and the old Roman Coliseum. The transition between styles was smooth but deliberate, the characteristics of both at times coming together to create something distinct from the individual contributions. It was quite the sight.

"Didn't hold anything back, did they?" came Casey's voice from behind him.

"Kind of intimidating, isn't it?" Monson heard Artorius remark.

Molly was the one who answered. "I think that's the point."

All three boys looked at her, puzzled.

"It all fits, if you think about it," she said, her eyes still on the building. "This school is the very definition of haughty. Some of the most renowned and talented minds of the last century have either studied or taught here. Very special people, my boys, more special than any of you could know. When you have special people, what better way to advertise than . . . well, this?"

She looked at the boys as she gestured at Coren's coliseum. "You take the good with the bad. There are some great things that are going to happen here for you, but keep your guard up."

Monson, Casey, and Artorius all looked at her with confusion etched on their faces. Molly noticed their expressions and said, "All I'm saying is that I'm glad the three of you met, Cassius, Artorius, and Monson. The three amigos. It has a sort of ring to it."

"Duh," Casey said, "they totally made a movie about it, but never mind that, how did you know—"

The massive doors of the modern coliseum opened, effectively silencing everyone in the crowd. A man walked toward them, a slight bounce in his step. He was approaching middle age, probably no more than forty, with a little gray in his short, dark hair, and an experienced look about him. He wore a crisp, dark suit and walked with confidence and energy and wore a contagious smile across his face. The man covered the distance to the new students quickly, though probably not quickly enough for the anxious crowd. He stopped in front of the nervous students.

"Welcome," the man said, giving some of the closer students a little wink. "I am Markin Gatt, a teacher here at Coren and your guide." He bowed slightly to all of them.

"I am here to take you the rest of the way, as the path ahead is somewhat treacherous," he said with a knowing smile.

The man scanned the crowd, still smiling, and lingered for a fraction of a second on Molly, but when Monson looked inquiringly at her, he saw no signs of recognition. Maybe he imagined it.

"Parents," the man was now calling out, "you will take the first right upon entering the Coliseum. Proceed up to the second balcony and take your seats there. You will be allowed to meet up with your children after the orientation."

At this announcement, Monson looked around at the parents, who were obviously annoyed, while most of the students looked disheartened at the thought of an assembly. The murmuring that had been rolling through the crowd subsided.

Mr. Gatt, apparently recognizing the looks of incredulity, smiled even wider. "It's tradition; the dean likes to talk to the students alone. He feels that this is a good time to begin the separation process."

"'Separation process?'" Casey said, raising an eyebrow. "What does that mean?"

Both Artorius and Monson shook their heads, and then all three of the boys looked at Molly. She half-heartedly smiled.

"Speaking of separation," Monson said, as something just then occurred to him, "where are your parents?"

This question received two very different reactions.

"My mom had to jet," Artorius said, unconcerned. "She wanted to be here, but she's a designer and has a show in Paris the day after tomorrow."

"My *guardians* couldn't make it today," Casey said, though he sounded a bit bitter. "Work, you know."

"Now, if there aren't any questions," Monson heard Mr. Gatt saying, "all the new students will follow me."

Monson, Artorius, and Casey picked up their belongings and followed the vast wave of students in front of them.

The students entered the building and followed Mr. Gatt down a series of hallways until they came to another set of double doors labeled "The Inner Chambers." Somehow the doors opened from the inside as the group approached. Everyone filed in, and instantly, excited muttering broke out.

The Inner Chambers were magnificent. The room was circular, with a large raised stage at the front. Boxed seating sat on raised platforms, which descended at even intervals to the middle of the oversized space, where a huge stage stood. Large silk banners bathed in crimson with the Coren University symbol traced in gold filigree hung from the ceiling, giving the space an earthy yet refined feel. The banisters, seats, and railways were built with beautifully carved wood that was deeply stained and polished with elaborate engravings of different scenes of nature. Inlaid lights offered direction for those finding their seats. The only thing that seemed out of place was the low ceiling directly above them.

On the center stage, a middle-aged man stood behind a large podium. He was handsome, with perfectly styled brown hair, steady brown eyes, high cheekbones, and white teeth. He looked like a newsperson—just a little too crisp to be real. He held himself with confidence and surveyed the students imperiously. Monson recognized the man but couldn't remember from where; it was another of those impressions that Monson was still getting used to. There were a few other people sitting rigidly behind the man. Still at a distance, the group behind the podium was difficult to see. Monson moved on, choosing to continue his observation of his immediate surroundings. He was sure he would have plenty of time to get to know the faculty. Now that they were actually in the room, Monson could see that the low bulging ceiling that felt so out of place upon their entrance was due to a series of elevated box seats and balconies. It made Monson wonder why they needed so much seating. There couldn't be enough students to fill this place. Where were all the people coming from?

The students moved slowly toward the front, taking seats close to the stage. Monson, Casey, and Artorius made their way down the third aisle from the front and parked themselves next to a large, frumpy-looking boy who smelled of cabbage. The boy turned from the friend with whom he had been talking as they approached. His eyes fell upon Artorius, Casey, and then Monson.

He stared openly at the scars on Monson's face. His eyes grew to the size of dinner plates. Monson didn't like the look in the boy's eyes —as if he recognized him. Quite suddenly, the boy turned back to his friend and spoke rapidly in an excited voice.

"Something really weird is going on," Monson said, leaning toward Casey. He looked at Casey inquisitively. "Do you have any idea what the *Horum Vir* is?"

"Well, of course I know what it is," Casey said indignantly, "but what does that have to do with . . . oh . . . I see . . .," he trailed off.

Monson just stared at him. Casey obviously understood something he didn't, so he waited. All at once, Casey spoke fast and excitedly. "But how could that have happened?!? The whole thing is fixed—everyone knows that."

"*What* are you talking about?" Monson's bewildered voice broke in.

"The *Horum Vir*," Casey's voice rose slightly. "That's the only way you could have made the Legion without trying out, *and* as a freshman. Oh man, can I pick friends! This is going to be sweet."

Monson interrupted. "Casey, hold up, what is a *Horum Vir*?"

"Not *what*," Casey said.

"OK," Monson said, a resigned note in his voice, "*who* is the *Horum Vir*?"

Monson already knew the answer. Casey placed his hand on Monson's shoulder and said, "You are, Monson."

CHAPTER 2
THE DEAN

THE DEAN of Coren University was standing placidly in front of the new students. He looked unruffled and regal as he started to speak. His hands were in just the right place, folded neatly in front of him, and he was neither fidgety nor nervous. It was obvious that he wanted to project a certain image right off the bat. The hall grew quiet as all eyes turned toward the dean.

"Welcome to Coren University." There was clapping and cheering from the upper decks. "I am Marcus Dayton, dean and headmaster of Coren University. This university follows in the proud tradition . . . ."

Monson could feel his eyes starting to droop. He pinched his own arm. Not a good idea to fall asleep during orientation.

"Now that we are all acquainted, I have a few announcements for you." The dean held up a small piece of paper. "I am very excited to tell you about some of the changes we've instituted this year."

Casey turned toward Monson. "He doesn't look very excited, does he?"

Monson focused on the dean's demeanor—haughty yet strained, handsome and the projection of perfect control, yet for some reason, Monson thought that he seemed ruffled just below the surface. His eyes shifted back and forth uneasily, like he was searching for some-thing. He seemed overly tense with no apparent reason.

The sound of his own name refocused his attention on the dean's long-forgotten speech.

"Is Mr. Grey here?" The dean's question sounded hopeful.

Casey prodded him to get up. "That's you, dude."

Monson rose slowly and felt dozens of eyes turn toward him. It was a disconcerting feeling and caused a strange strain on his disjointed memory.

Bright lights, cameras, people—so many people. Cheers, but what were they cheering for? A stage. Disappointment followed by anger. Soft voices and a warming sensation that blocked everything else. The warmth enveloped him.

The images rolled over Monson but abruptly changed.

Screams. Blood. Pain. Anger. Hatred. So much hatred. Hatred turned to bloodlust, just to be replaced by darkness.

Monson glared inwardly as he forced himself to catch hold of the thoughts streaming through him. One memory jumped to the front, and he remembered! He remembered the night he won the scholarship to this blasted school. He felt happy at the breakthrough, yet troubled by the change in the memory. The screaming. The blood. The pain and anger. That—that was new.

That whole period, actually *every* period before the incident on Baroty Bridge, was still hazy. The competition had happened right before it. Details still evaded him, but he did not need details, as many thoughts began clicking into place in Monson's mind.

The Knowledge Bowl, the *Horum Vir* scholarship . . . they were connected. No, not just connected . . . the *Horum Vir* thing and that competition . . . they were the same thing! It all made sense. He was the winner of the Coren University *Horum Vir* competition—the most highly coveted academic scholarship in the world of secondary educa-tion. He was the new *Horum Vir*. Monson thought back to the long conversations with Molly concerning his big opportunity to go to a good school. Molly had obviously known about all of it the entire time. No wonder she didn't tell him.

Monson grumbled inwardly. *Molly, you are so dead! What else have you been hiding from me?*

Brimming with irritation, Monson scanned the less-than-inconspicuous glances of his soon-to-be classmates when a face jumped out at him.

Waves of golden blonde hair tied in a half ponytail partially hid the face of a girl with a pair of cool green eyes that were steady and unflinching as they connected with his. Monson and the girl looked at each other for a moment, and then her gaze flickered to either side of him like she was searching for something.

That's the girl Molly pointed out in the parking lot earlier, Monson thought, recognizing the girl. She was sitting a couple of rows in front of him and to the right, surrounded by a crowd of both female and male students, all jockeying for her attention. She responded to the girls but seemed to take little interest in what they had to say. She took even less interest in the boys that were trying to catch her eye.

Casey again leaned toward Monson. "Kylie Coremack."

"What?" Monson said absent-mindedly.

"Her name is Kylie Coremack." Casey gestured toward the girl. "She attended St. Brown with Artorius and me, though she's a year older. She went to some school in Spain last year. I don't know why she decided to come here now. Can't say I'm surprised, though. It's just like her to change her mind and inconvenience her whole—" He stopped suddenly, looking distracted. He righted himself, continuing in a more controlled voice, "Her family is old money and is very much a part of the upper crust. And if you couldn't tell, her personality leaves you wanting."

"Leaves you wanting?" Monson did not understand. "What does that mean?"

"I mean her personality leaves you wanting . . . to get away from her."

"She's cute, though." Artorius craned his neck to get a look at her. "Always been cute."

"Yeah, with all the compassion of a fence post," Casey retorted, a slight edge in his voice. "And not even a particularly nice fence post."

Monson's eyebrow shot up. "Casey, I'm not sure that makes any sense. Are nice fence posts known for their compassion?"

Casey glared at Monson. The look made Monson cower a bit.

Monson turned and caught Artorius' eye. The big redhead shook his head and silently mouthed, "I'll explain later."

The boys returned their attention to the dean, who was droning on about the high standards expected at Coren, free time, and leaving the campus. He rounded off his speech with a discussion of The Legion. Monson's new friends did not mention Kylie again. While she was obviously a sore subject, Monson noticed that Casey continued to cast covert glances at her. Monson's gut told him that Casey's situation was more complex than a simple matter of haughty disdain. Interesting, indeed.

"I want you all to appreciate how important competition is to the faculty and sponsors here at Coren. Understand that this school is the standard in secondary education and the resources expended on our behalf are vast. Failure is not tolerated." The dean looked around imperiously, stopping for a fraction of a second longer on Monson. "You should be aware of the happenings at Coren. Expulsion is something that is used here with frequentness."

Casey snickered. "Is that even a word?" he asked, turning toward Monson and Artorius.

"I think so." Monson scratched his chin. "Sounds pretty funny in that sentence though, doesn't it?"

"I think *frequency* is what he's looking for."

"Or *frequently*," Monson pointed out.

They debated that point until the end of Dean Dayton's speech. As they talked, other people that had been stationed behind the dean, including Coach Able, the Legion's coach, came forward to speak.

Coach Able, a small, frumpy-looking man, headed the Athletics and Academic Support Departments. Monson didn't listen to him.

Different department heads followed Coach Able, all spewing a never-ending dribble of noise. Granted, the boys did not actually listen to any of them, but they were still completely bored.

Everyone was hopeful the speeches were over when finally the dean returned to the podium. "I want you all to remember that we support each other at this school. My door is always open; I encourage you to use it."

Yeah right. Monson examined the way the dean's jaw constricted as he said this. *I'm sure you are just **dying** for us to come see you.*

"That's a P.R. dance if I've ever seen one," Casey noted.

"Yeah," Monson agreed. "Remind me to never seek his advice."

The dean, after a round of polite applause, left the stage. Many of the students clapped only a couple of times before they went back to conversing among themselves. Yet the speeches continued. Some administrative advisors spoke at length about classes, the support system, dorms, and "interpersonal relations."

"Does she mean like dating?" Casey asked, amused as a rigid-looking woman spoke solemnly about propriety and discretion. "Why did she refer to it as 'interpersonal relations?'"

"Who knows," Monson said. "Maybe it embarrasses her?"

"What a thought," Casey said.

After the painful speech about interpersonal relations, Mr. Gatt, who looked just as bored as everyone else in the room, jumped up to the podium.

"Now, if all of you will stand up and make your way to my left, I will show you to your dormitory. Parents, you can follow Eden." He pointed up toward the balcony to a man standing off to the side. "He will show you where you can meet back up with your students."

The students stood up and mulled about for a few moments before they gathered their luggage and slowly started to move toward the doors.

Artorius and Casey resumed their conversation about football. Monson, not knowing much about the subject, let his concentration roam as the crowd of people steered him and his companions down the light-studded path. A flicker caught Monson's eye, and he saw a shimmer of light gleaming off glossy black hair. It was gone before he understood what it was. Monson tried to get a better look, tried to find the source of the light, but in his eagerness was not paying attention. He tripped and triggered a chain reaction that sent students flying in every direction.

It was pandemonium! Luggage and people tumbled everywhere. Monson rolled several steps until he landed on something soft. There were groans and moans coming from all around as people tried to figure out what had happened. Monson heard Casey behind him, his voice a mix of horror and suppressed laughter.

"Grey, are you OK?"

Monson did not answer. He could not answer. A pure and sweet smell enveloped his senses, making him lightheaded. There was something wrong here. Monson opened his eyes. Revelation came swiftly and with all the force of a blunt ax when a voice, muffled and distraught, said, "Do you think you could get off of me, please?"

Monson shook the fuzziness from his head and saw tousled waves of blonde hair coming loose from a disheveled half-ponytail. Kylie Coremack gazed at him with soft green orbs. She whispered quietly, "You're hurting my back."

People moved around them. Seeing this, Kylie's quiet reserve bloomed into full demon mode. She flipped a switch, and calm understanding evolved into hateful disgust.

"Oh, sorry." Monson scrambled to his feet. "I didn't . . . I wasn't . . .," he trailed off, not really knowing what to say.

"Oh, I see," she said with a surprising amount of sympathy as she stood unassisted. "You weren't paying attention to where you were going, right?"

Monson started to squirm. The crowd of girls that had been sitting with Kylie during the dean's presentation started to move in behind her. Many of them were bearing minor injuries. Obviously, they too had suffered from Monson's misstep. They stood behind Kylie, whispering behind hands and shooting him venomous looks.

"Yeah," Monson said finally, trying to keep the nervousness out of his voice. "I wasn't paying attention. I'm really sorry I knocked you over."

"You're *sorry,*" she said this time without a trace of sympathy. "You are . . . sorry. Oh, well, if you are *sorry.*" Monson could hear the venom in her voice now.

She paused. "Do you realize what you have done?" She was yelling now, an angry flush starting to creep up her neck and face.

"No . . . should I?" Monson asked, bewildered.

Behind Kylie, different girls clapped their hands to their mouths, looking scandalized. Kylie's face completed the morph, growing angrier and angrier. As her face started to contort, her skin went blotchy. Monson could see the stress lines forming at the base of her neck. She opened her mouth. Nothing came out. Apparently, the severity of his crime was so gruesome, it left her momentarily speechless. Abruptly, as if an imaginary dam burst within her, Kylie bellowed while pointing to a spot over Monson's shoulder. "DAMION'S FIRST IMPRESSION! YOU RUINED IT!" With this statement, many of the girls behind Kylie started to look around wildly, and then, as one, looked over Monson's right shoulder.

On an adjacent building from a side balcony overlooking Monson and the assortment of girls stood about a dozen boys watching with amusement on their faces. Monson turned and looked straight into the face of a boy who appeared to be the leader, as all the others seemed to be waiting on his reaction. Monson recognized him immediately: Damion Peterson, "The Diamond." That boy . . . the one he beat in the Knowledge Bowl. When he became the new *Horum Vir.*

Monson stared for a moment, disbelief etched on his face. Not only did he remember the boy's face, but also some details about him. The boy was a star, probably one of the most talented athletes the school had ever seen, but he was also on scholarship, right? How did he get back in? How could he afford it? The Diamond looked at Monson for a moment. His expression was unrecognizable. That moment felt like a lifetime for Monson. They just stood eyeing each other.

Damion broke their eye contact and gestured to his friends, who started to move toward the back of the balcony.

"I only had one chance to make a first impression," Kylie said, her attention snapping back to Monson, who gave a little start. He had almost forgotten her. She continued, "I will never get another chance to make a good first impression on Damion."

She straightened herself up, and those frosty bluish-green eyes seemed to crackle with electricity. "And YOU, in turn, will never get another chance to impress *me*. I hope you're happy."

She stormed off, her gang of girls in tow, toward the exit where Mr. Gatt was still waiting. The audience of students, who until now stood captivated, caused another uproar in their haste to get out of the way of the enraged girl. Many people, unsure of whom they should stare at, gaped back and forth between Monson and Kylie Coremack, delighted at the drama unfolding before them.

Monson felt winded, unsure if he should laugh or be upset at the turn of events. He turned to Casey, who appeared more serious than Monson could have imagined. An edgy, almost dangerous look inched its way onto his face. Artorius just grimaced.

Someone touched Monson on the back. He turned swiftly, expecting to see some new impending disaster dropped at his feet. Mr. Gatt stood calmly in front of him. With no pretense or greeting, he simply said, "Well, Mr. Grey, it appears we are going to have to work on your people skills."

CHAPTER 3
A GIFT

"YOU CERTAINLY HAVE a way with the ladies, Mr. Grey," Mr. Gatt said ten minutes later. Artorius and Casey laughed. It helped to ease the potent tension still pooling from their encounter with Kylie. Mr. Gatt had handed off the large body of students to other faculty members and was now accompanying the *Horum Vir* and his companions. Monson really didn't need the personal escort but was reluctant to say anything.

Monson scowled at Mr. Gatt's remark. "Honestly, the way she was yelling at me, you would have thought I just murdered her cat or something."

"That's just how she is," Artorius said, still chuckling. "You should have seen when Casey and she got into it last—"

"Ar-*thur*!" Casey shot out angrily. "We really don't need to talk about that."

"Oh, come on," Artorius replied, a malicious grin on his face. "It's in the past. You need to let it go, my man."

"Yeah, Casey," Monson said. "What's with the two of you? And don't try to deny it. You guys have a past. Spill it."

"Now is not the time or the place," Casey said, giving Mr. Gatt a sideways glance.

Mr. Gatt chuckled. "Please, do not let me stop you. As a matter of fact, I'm fairly curious myself. I like to know what motivates my students."

This was obviously not what Casey wanted to hear. "It's such a long, boring story." He looked flushed and uncomfortable.

Monson opened his mouth to encourage him, but before he could say anything, Mr. Gatt cut him off.

"Do not worry, lad. This is not something that has to be shared now. Perhaps another time."

Casey looked at him, relief starting to dull the red color that had overtaken his face. The group pressed on, picking up their pace a bit.

Mr. Gatt did not talk much as he led the three boys to their dormitory. This was perfectly fine with Monson; the quiet was not something that bothered him. Casey chatted up a storm, telling Artorius about his summer, the places he had visited, the girls he had met, and a bundle of other things, all of which sounded exaggerated. Artorius seemed content to listen as Casey dived headlong into a story about a trip to Rome. Monson stopped listening and turned his attention to Mr. Gatt.

"So, how long have you worked here, Mr. Gatt?" Monson asked politely.

To Monson's surprise, Mr. Gatt let out an ironic laugh. Monson observed, but did not comment, that it was probably a good thing Mr. Gatt had not been drinking at that moment, as something would have come flying out of his nose. Mr. Gatt certainly was a strange man. He continued laughing for a minute or so, then, wiping a tear from his eye, said, "Well, young man, that is quite the question, and I suppose it depends on what you mean."

This was not the answer Monson had expected.

"I am not sure what *you* mean, Mr. Gatt. I—"

Mr. Gatt interrupted him.

"My apologies. My own little joke." He cleared his throat. "I guess I was inquiring if you wanted to know how long I've *actually* been here, or how long it *feels* like I've been here."

Monson looked perplexed. "Well, I guess I mean how long you've actually been here."

"About twenty-five years, off and on," he said simply.

Now Monson was thoroughly confused. He did not understand what was so funny about working at Coren for twenty-five years. He also could not help but feel amazed. Mr. Gatt did not look that old. His hair threw you off, but up close, his face boasted late thirties at the most.

Markin Gatt looked at him, a fatherly expression on his face. "Mr. Grey... Monson, this is a world of privilege, and with those privileges, there are certain expectations and norms one must follow."

"So, why is that funny?" Monson asked timidly, not wanting to offend.

"Allow me to answer in the form of a question," Mr. Gatt said patiently. "What happens in a society that is highly restricted by rules and regulations when someone within that society does not conform?"

"I have no idea," Monson said plainly. "That person is thrown out?"

Markin Gatt laughed again. "In a way. Their interactions are definitely constricted. However, they are not thrown out, especially in a society like this one." He stopped for a second, spun around on the balls of his feet, and pointed to the surroundings. "These people," Mr. Gatt continued, "would not physically throw anyone out; it is not en vogue."

Monson raised an eyebrow. He was not sure what Mr. Gatt was talking about. *Who are these people?*

"Do not worry, my friend. You're a bright one. You'll eventually understand what I'm talking about, but it's a lesson that you'll need to learn early, I'm afraid: appropriate responses for the appropriate situation."

Monson could not think of anything to say in answer to that and thought a change in subject might be warranted.

"You said that you've been here off and on for twenty-five years, right?"

"Yes, that is correct."

"What were you doing when you weren't teaching?"

"Adventuring."

Monson blinked, certain that he must have heard wrong.

"Adventuring?"

"Have you ever seen any of the Indiana Jones films?"

Actually, Monson had seen the first movie. It was a good flick.

He looked at Mr. Gatt suspiciously.

"I've seen one of those movies. Why do you ask?"

"Consider me a real-life Dr. Jones." He looked rather satisfied with himself. "That's what I do when I'm not here. It is all very exciting."

"Then why are you back here?" Monson wondered, since it was pretty obvious that he found this place distasteful. The question was simple but seemed important.

"Research," Mr. Gatt answered rather lamely.

"Research?" Monson asked. "What sort of research?"

Mr. Gatt smiled. "I'm looking for someone."

Monson smiled back. "A woman? You should try eHarmony. I hear it works wonders."

Mr. Gatt laughed as he picked up his pace but offered no more details. Regardless, Monson felt his curiosity prickle. Mr. Gatt was indeed an interesting one.

The walk to the dorms seemed to take almost no time at all, even though Monson knew it was on the other side of Coren's sizable campus. The grounds displayed an abundance of the now-recognizable stylized architecture he first noticed in Coren's Coliseum. The structures were enormous, beautiful, and clearly expensive; it was not difficult to understand what impression Coren's board of directors was determined to make. However, something was lost in the overall effect. To Monson, much of it seemed too planned and rigid.

After about ten or fifteen minutes of walking, Monson, Mr. Gatt,

Artorius, and Casey all arrived at a massive and bulky structure with elegant decor. White brick walkways lined with lighted stone columns perfectly matched the gray sculpted stone of the building's exterior, including an indoor atrium visible from any walkway. A large hedge encircled the building, giving it a secretive feeling, as if this place was a world apart from the rest, a refuge of some sort.

Mr. Gatt, moving quickly, continued to walk until he came to a three-way fork in the walkway. Preceding the fork, ever so slightly, was a large, finely carved stone arch. He stopped directly under the arch and turned to look at the three boys.

"Welcome to The Barracks, boys," Mr. Gatt said in a formal voice while bowing. "I will now show the *Horum Vir* to his prepared quarters."

Monson, Casey, and Artorius exchanged inquisitive looks, taken aback by Mr. Gatt's formal manner. Monson recovered first.

"Mr. Gatt," he said, sounding unsure. "Why exactly are you talking like that?"

Mr. Gatt gave Monson a warm smile and put his hand on Monson's shoulder. With a little squeeze, he replied, "I am sorry about that. I guess it is a habit. There is supposed to be a kind of ceremony called the 'Induction.' It is when the students and parents meet in the indoor atrium to see the *Horum Vir* and his 'Ascension' into his quarters." He took his hand off Monson and placed it on his own chest. "I am usually the Master of Ceremonies at the Induction. The formality is a hard habit to break."

"That's weird." Casey stepped away from the arch and moved a bit closer to both Monson and Mr. Gatt. He looked around, tracing the stone walkway with his eyes as if to see if there were people hiding in the bushes. "What the hell happened to the ceremony this year?"

"Do not swear, Cassius," chided Mr. Gatt. "It's a sign of a weak mind and an undisciplined tongue."

Casey looked taken aback. "Sorry."

"Monson's winning of the *Horum Vir* scholarship was something of a surprise," continued Mr. Gatt. "The Induction ceremony was canceled because the board was unsure whether Monson was going to claim the scholarship. The ceremony is quite elaborate, with celebrities, political figures, and businessmen from all over. It's very much a spectacle. The Board didn't have time to organize on the timeline Mr. Grey here gave them. But do not fret; there will be a small reception this evening."

"There you are!"

It was Molly. She jogged up to the small group, looking slightly winded. "Molly!" Monson said, moving toward her to steady her. "Are you all right?"

"Hey there, love," she finally said after catching her breath. "I'm fine. I'm just glad I didn't miss you. I was going to wait for you just outside the Coliseum, but I realized they weren't having the ceremony this year."

"What, did you think I was going to let you leave without saying goodbye?" Monson answered. "Don't be silly."

Molly smiled at his pitiful attempt at humor. "You're such a sweet boy. I'm going to miss you."

"Me too," Monson said fondly. It was true. He *was* going to miss her. She had been his rock for the past few months, one of the only connections to his past, and for a time, his only friend. Monson suddenly felt sad; he was going to miss this woman a great deal more than he had been willing to admit.

Molly smiled at him again, her eyes shiny. She surprised him when she gently laid her hand on his face, lightly touching his scars. She kissed him on the forehead. Monson looked at her. Molly never displayed this kind of affection.

As if this was not weird enough, Monson received another shock when he heard a slight sniff. Confused, he looked into her big, dark eyes and gasped. Tears were starting to flow liberally, making her eyes and cheeks puff. She sniffed again. He looked to Artorius and Casey. They just stared back at Monson, obviously more confused than he was.

"Molly..." Monson tried to keep the concern and confusion out of his voice.

"Shhhh," she said softly. She pulled a small bag out of her pocket and gestured for Monson to take it. "Monson, honey, I have a gift for you. It's something very important to your family, so I want you to promise me that you will always wear it."

Monson took the small cloth bag and opened it. It contained a small square box, the same type that would hold an engagement ring or anniversary gift. Monson held up the box and then said with some bravado, "Are you asking for my hand in marriage, Molly? Because I'm flattered, but I'm not sure I'm your type."

Everyone laughed, including Molly. This went on for a moment and helped to relieve some of the tension. Molly, still giggling, said, "Just open the box, smartass."

Monson did just that and gawked as he beheld a large, silver stone set on a silver chain. Monson looked at Molly in disbelief.

"Well," Molly said, her voice becoming less emotional and more dignified, "examine it. Get to know each other."

On this enigmatic note, Monson scrutinized the stone, removing it from its box. More a gem than a mere stone, its color was a deep silver, but seemingly transparent as well. Mesmerized, Monson lifted the stone to the light of the sun and searched its depths.

Strange. The distance within the stone seemed incomprehensible and changing, like the material just below the surface was constantly shifting. He lowered his arm and smiled. This stone was one of the most mysterious and beautiful things Monson had ever seen.

"It was your grandfather's," Molly whispered. "He told me to hang on to it. I want you to take very good care of it. It's a gift from him."

"Molly, I—" Monson stammered, but Molly just put a finger to her lips.

"Well, then, let's see it on," she said with some of her former excitement. She gestured for him to return it. He gave it back to her and turned around. After another moment, a silver chain appeared around his neck, the stone hanging in the middle. It was in that exact moment that Monson finally felt at ease for the first time in a very long while. It was strange, but something about Molly's demeanor, her formality, and even the stone itself gave him a feeling of hope. That feeling, which had been lost to him for some time, was bittersweet. Monson smiled as he looked from the stone around his neck to his two new friends, to Mr. Gatt, and then finally to Molly. As corny as it sounded, he was glad they were all there.

There was nothing left to say. Monson smiled and then put out his hand to shake Molly's, who was looking relieved for some reason. Abandoning all pretenses, she threw her arms around him and squeezed as if her life depended on it.

"I'm so proud of you. Hardships await, but you'll rise to the task. I know you will. Be courageous and happy."

Molly released him. He, in turn, hugged her again.

"I'll see you at Christmas."

"Of course," Molly said, pulling away and wiping her eyes. "Have a good term." With that farewell, she started toward the other side of the campus and the parking lot. After a short distance, she turned and waved energetically, beaming. It was odd, but something told Monson that he was not the only one to whom she was waving.

———

"YOU AND YOUR mom have a really weird relationship." Casey looked perplexed. The look on his face made Monson snicker.

"Oh!" Monson smacked his forehead. "I forgot you wouldn't know."

"I wouldn't know what?"

"Molly isn't my mother."

"OK... then who is she?"

"My lawyer."

Everyone except Monson burst out laughing. This continued for a while until they noticed that Monson was not joining in.

"You're serious?" Artorius said.

"It's a really long story, and it's kind of depressing, so let's not talk about it right now."

"Fair enough," Casey said, picking up his luggage.

"OK, but I want to hear this story, so don't forget to tell us," Artorius said.

"Why are you so interested in Molly?" Monson asked, flummoxed.

"She was crying," Artorius said, something close to wonderment in his voice.

"Yeah, what does that have to do with anything?"

"My dad is a lawyer," Artorius answered, "and I wasn't aware that lawyers could cry."

They all laughed this time.

"Mr. Gatt," Casey said, moving toward him. "I believe you were going to show us where we're staying."

"That I was, Mr. Kay," he replied with a bow. "If you will please follow me."

They gathered all their stuff once more and moved through the arch and down the center pathway toward the Atrium.

"This is your entrance," Mr. Gatt explained, looking over to Monson. "It makes it a lot easier than trying to navigate the boys' or girls' dormitories."

Mr. Gatt took the boys through large glass double doors and started up a red brick path toward the center of the Atrium. The boys followed, marveling at their surroundings, including some expertly crafted stonework.

"Wow!" Monson said as he moved through the Atrium. "That's amazing."

There were statues—a lot of them: stone depictions of heroes and heroines, gods and goddesses, all on the bottom floor of the student dorm. At the center was a large and grandiose foundation with hundreds of spouting veins of water that arced and rippled in a variety of paths. As if this wasn't enough, on top of the fountain stood the statue of a giant, probably twenty-five feet tall and weighing at least a couple of tons. The features of the statue were finely shaped, especially the eyes. Spotlights illuminated his perch, forcing the eye to this spot in the Atrium.

"Jupiter," Mr. Gatt said simply.

"Ahh," Monson said, comprehension finally hitting him. *Of course. Who better than the king of the gods to watch over the students?* he thought. *The old myths and legends of antiquity were one of the things Monson enjoyed most about history. The gods especially were of interest to him. Monson asked himself more than once what it would be like to have almost infinite power at your fingertips and still have all the imperfections and contradictions that are so much a part of the human condition. He had heard the saying that absolute power corrupts absolutely. Monson wondered if that was true.*

He took a step closer and examined the fine detail and the smooth marble. He really liked this statue.

"So, who is this guy supposed to be?" Casey asked, obviously bored.

"Jupiter," Artorius answered.

"How did you know that?" Casey asked, sounding slightly surprised.

"Well," Artorius said, starting to grin. "The huge thunderbolt kind of gave it away. Then, of course, there was the whole part where Mr. Gatt just said it was Jupiter."

Monson thought he heard Mr. Gatt stifle a laugh, though when he spoke, his voice sounded quite level.

"Over here, please. The *Horum Vir's* entrance is right around the corner."

Casey and Artorius grabbed their stuff and started after Mr. Gatt. Monson, however, stood for a moment more, staring at the stunning sculpture. He looked up into the blank, staring face of Jupiter, king of the gods, and shuddered.

"Absolute power..." He placed a hand on his chin and stared

directly into the face of the statue. "So how did that work out for you, Jupiter, old boy? It's lonely at the top, no? Well, if it makes you feel any better, it ain't that great at the bottom either."

Monson winked. Why he winked at an inanimate object, he wasn't sure. He just felt inclined to do so, and obviously, the statue felt the same way: It winked back at him.

Monson froze. That did not just happen.

"Monson! Hurry up or we're going to be late." Casey's voice sounded a short distance off.

Monson called after him, keeping his eyes on Jupiter, "Late? Late for what?" Nothing came in response.

Monson tore his eyes from the king of the Roman gods and hurried after the others.

———

THE ENTRANCE to the *Horum Vir*'s quarters was a small elevator found in one of the corners of the Atrium. It was a little cramped, but after a few minutes of arranging, Monson, Casey, Artorius, Mr. Gatt, and all the luggage were packed in the elevator and cruising upward to the top floor of The Barracks. Cramped and uncomfortable, talking seemed like a luxury they could forgo. After a few sore moments, in which everyone wished wholeheartedly that they had split up, the elevator screeched to a halt and the doors opened. This caused everyone and everything except Mr. Gatt to tumble out of the elevator. Being the closest to the door, Monson fell first. He spilled forward, hitting the ground hard. He looked up just as Artorius and Casey lost their balance. Monson shuddered as they came stumbling out after him.

In the midst of the disorder, an odd-looking man rushed to their side, catching them all off-guard. He was skinny to the point of bony, with long fingers, high cheekbones, and thin eyebrows. He also had a kind of austere manner that spoke of an unwavering strictness. Despite this, he looked at them with kind eyes that were brown with hints of green.

"Ah, Brian," said Mr. Gatt, putting his hand forward. "I was wondering where you scampered off to."

"Markin," Brian said, extending his own hand and shaking Mr. Gatt's vigorously. "It has taken you a great deal longer than I expected. I thought you might be in the Comfort Room with the other students and parents. So I went to investigate."

"What did you find?"

Brian shrugged elegantly. "The usual pretentious people, of course."

"Well, allow me to alleviate that burden," Mr. Gatt replied, letting out a slight chuckle. "Let me introduce you to the new *Horum Vir*, Monson Grey."

"Hero," Brian said, giving Monson a slight bow. "I am very glad to make your acquaintance."

"Hero?" Monson said, confused by the greeting. "Why are you calling me Hero?"

Brian looked slightly shocked. "Hero—have you not been told what '*Horum Vir*' means?"

"No, I don't think so," Monson replied.

"*Horum Vir* is Latin for hero. Well, actually, *the* Hero."

Monson raised an eyebrow. "So, I get to walk around with everyone calling me Hero? Nice. Now if you'll excuse me, I think I'm going to throw myself off a balcony."

"I see this one has a quick wit," Brian noted.

"And a sharp tongue. I think you're going to have your hands full with him, my old friend."

"Indeed."

Monson glared at the two men. "On behalf of all teenagers, I just wanted to let you know that we love it when you talk about us as if we aren't here. We think it's awesome."

Mr. Gatt put up a hand. "Peace, Monson, we're on your side, I assure you."

Brian bowed. "Please allow me to show you to your quarters. You're in for quite the treat."

"You two, please follow me," Mr. Gatt said to Casey and Artorius. "I'll show you where you'll be staying."

"You got it!" Casey said buoyantly to Mr. Gatt as he finished gathering his scattered possessions. "We'll hook up with you later... *Hero.*" He looked highly amused.

CHAPTER 4
DREAMS

BRIAN GATHERED up Monson's things and then led him down another highly ornate hallway. Covered in murals, the length of the passage displayed an assortment of Roman military ventures, some historical and others obviously fictional. The murals showed remarkable artistic skill. The soldiers and their commanders remained locked in eternal combat with hordes of barbarians and charlatans, as the fury of the Roman war machine devastated lines of blurred figures in the background. The illustrations suited this hall well. It felt like a culmination of ideas that described the school and the attitudes of a long-forgotten people suddenly reborn in the modern. This mural was Coren and Rome personified in an epic artistic rendition.

"I have never liked these paintings," Brian said, looking at the murals with distaste.

"Really?" asked Monson with some surprise. "Why is that?"

"Actually, to be completely honest with you, I've never liked the whole Roman concept," Brian replied. "Granted, it's not like it originated with their society; there has always been such. Probably always will be. The Romans aren't anything special in that particular regard."

"I'm not quite sure I understand."

"My dear young Hero," Brian said patiently. "What—"

He paused, considering his words. "Let me answer you in the form of a question. Were the Romans great, and if that be the case, for what reason?"

Monson scrutinized Brian, trying to discern his possible meaning. He knew there was a specific answer that Brian was looking for but had no idea what it was.

"Yes," Monson answered, acting more confident than he felt, but also thinking he had an indisputable fact that proved their greatness.

Brian's face reflected a polite interest that plainly told Monson to go on. Monson obliged, "I think you need to look at all the different things they were responsible for. I mean, if you think about it, there is hardly an area of science, philosophy, or religion that the Romans didn't have at least some influence over."

"Yes, that is true," Brian said with a wry smile. "But how were they able to accomplish all of those great things?"

Monson paused for a moment, unsure of the question's meaning. Brian gave him an understanding smile. "Let me ask you this: Do you think the *people* the Romans conquered thought they were great?"

The answer was obvious.

"Probably not," Monson answered tentatively.

"Exactly." Brian looked amused. "Yes, we have many great things from the Romans. Their accomplishments were far-reaching, even everlasting, but their crimes were just as, if not more, far-reaching and everlasting. Always remember, winners are the ones who write the history. There are two sides to every story, but more often than not, we are only party to one side."

"I guess I never really thought about it," Monson commented, taken aback.

"It certainly does make you think, does it not? History is supposed to be about the truth and facts. One should not be illustrating any particular action in any particular light, but instead relaying events and analyzing observable facts." Brian gestured toward the wall. "Now

58

answer me this, young Master Grey: What if the artist had been able to immortalize the innocent people who died in both battle and siege? The women and children who lost fathers, husbands, and brothers in the fury of pointless conflict, or the pain suffered by those who had lost all hope, faith, and the will to live because of a cause they neither knew nor understood? Now *that* would be a picture worthy of admiration."

"Brian," Monson said, again puzzled, "what exactly do you do here?"

"Oh, I apologize, where are my manners?!" Brian chuckled. "I started to ramble." He adopted a slightly more formal tone, one that sounded a great deal like Mr. Gatt. "My dear Hero, I am thy manservant."

Monson thought he heard wrong. "I'm sorry. You're my what?"

"Thy manservant."

"And what the bloody hell is that?" Monson said, exasperated. Why did it seem that everyone at this school was reluctant to give him a straight answer?

"As *Horum Vir*, you are given certain privileges and responsibilities." Brian adjusted the bags he was carrying for Monson and smoothly pulled out a small envelope, removed a blue key card, and stopped in front of a great oak door.

"I am at the same time a privilege and responsibility. I am here to make sure that you fulfill your responsibilities and that you take full advantage of your privileges."

"Responsibilities?" Monson grimaced. "That sounds awfully unpleasant."

"Yes, responsibilities can be unpleasant." Brian winked at him. "Then again, privileges can more than make up for this."

In one fluid motion, the door opened without a sound.

"Whoa," was all Monson said as Brian slid through and stepped aside. Monson followed. He was instantly impressed.

Monson walked into a handsome sitting area where oversized leather chairs and a sofa were carefully arranged around a sturdy oak coffee table. Sizable floor lamps stood on either side of the chairs, dousing the area with mounds of soft light. Adjacent to the sitting area was a large wooden entertainment center, completely self-contained behind wooden shutters. On the other side of the room, a double window covered by a handsome shade of horizontal slats sat between two sets of double doors.

"Welcome to your quarters." Brian set the bags down and walked over to the window. He opened it to reveal a breathtaking view of the grounds and national forest at the edge of Coren's property. "This is where you'll be staying during your time here. Feel free to explore."

Monson was happy to oblige.

He moved freely, stopping periodically when he found something of interest. He noticed that besides the sitting area, which could easily be used for entertaining, there was a wet bar, complete with a refrigerator and an assortment of labor-saving appliances. Upon closer inspection, he realized the wet bar was more akin to a small kitchen, and although it wasn't large, it appeared to be fairly well equipped. He also noticed a control panel with commands such as "lights," "music," and "movies." Monson suspected this was a sort of voice-activated feature, as there weren't any buttons, just a large speaker located in the middle of the panel. It was all very cool.

"Brian, what can you tell me about this position that I have?" Monson walked to one of the plush leather chairs and sat down, looking at Brian intently. "In one day I've gone from being the winner of a scholarship to attending a school—a good school—but a school nonetheless, to being a rock star. You spoke of the responsibilities; what exactly are they expecting me to do?"

"Master Grey," Brian bowed slightly, "I would be happy to enlighten you, but not right now. You still have many things to do. You need to eat something and rest."

He turned back to Monson. "Though I am curious, why did you not read the information packet you received after you won the Knowledge Bowl?"

Monson flushed. He really didn't want to talk about that.

"It's a long story."

Brian did not pursue the subject but rather beckoned Monson to follow him. He walked to the left side of the room to one set of double oak doors, and with a flick of his wrist, opened them to reveal Monson's bedroom. And what a bedroom it was.

It was spacious, but not ostentatiously so. A massive four-poster bed carved of redwood, complete with silk hangings, dominated the center of the room. A nightstand and dresser to either side of the marvelous bed completed the picture. A half-opened doorway directly to Monson's left revealed a huge bathroom. To the right was a large bay window. Monson looked around the room in awe. What kind of lives were these people living that they could offer such opulence to one such as he?

Brian was next to the bed parting the curtains.

One look at a fluffy comforter and mountains of pillows, and Monson lost his self-control. He ran and jumped, spinning in mid-air to land on his back in the center of the bed. He kicked off his shoes as he sunk into the mattress.

Brian gave a smile and an appreciative chuckle. "You and I are going to get along just fine, lad. I'll get you something to eat, and then you should get a bit of rest."

"Rest?" asked Monson, surprised. "Like sleep? *Now*? Aren't there other things I should be attending to, like meeting teachers or something?"

"Most of the other students are getting to know their roommates right now," Brian replied, his voice calm and reassuring. "About an hour is allocated to this portion of the orientation. You can go and introduce yourself to the various Floor Captains if you wish."

"No, that's all right," Monson said, ignoring the fact that he had no idea what a Floor Captain was.

"You look quite tired. Relax for a moment, and I'll bring you something to eat."

Monson relented, acknowledging Brian with a nod.

Brian gave another slight bow and left, closing the great double doors behind him.

What a nice...weirdo, Monson thought to himself. Between Brian and Mr. Gatt, Monson wasn't going to run out of adults to annoy.

Adults. Monson found that he suddenly missed Molly. He indulged in a back-cracking stretch and thought he would take Brian's advice and rest for a while. He was tired from the excitement of the day; a short snooze would do him some good. He slowly moved to the top of the bed to pull down the covers, which were tucked far under the headboard. As he pulled back the blankets and sheets, his thoughts wandered to Kylie Coremack and her little speech. He wondered if that type of behavior was normal for girls. He really hoped not. A verbal lashing like that was a once-in-a-lifetime experience, and not one he would readily repeat. The situation didn't make sense to him. Her change in attitude and demeanor—it was so sudden and felt forced, though that didn't really make sense. Why put on a show like that?

Monson looked at the uncovered bed. Suddenly, he didn't want to sleep but thought he would instead check out the rest of his apartment.

Monson went directly for the only door that remained unopened, crossing the entire apartment to get there. The door revealed a handsome office, complete with an oak computer desk. More of the plush furniture—an L-shaped couch and armchair—sat to either side of an expansive bookshelf that reached from floor to ceiling.

Monson went to a chair sitting in front of the desk. He reclined briefly before he noticed a rippled cover that hid most of the desk's surface. Monson searched and found a small button under the lip of the desktop. He pushed it, and the cover retracted with a slight clink. To Monson's delight, an expensive-looking computer complete with a flat, high-definition screen, a scanner, and a printer sat on the desktop. Monson smiled appreciatively as he slid the shade back into place.

Getting up, his attention wandered to the large shelf of books along the wall. Before the attack, Monson read—a lot. This was one of the things that his grandfather had encouraged. Never stop learning, he would say. It was odd that this, of all things, he remembered, but he did remember, with surprising clarity. Words are power, his grandfather had said, and reading along with developing skills of reason is the key to unlocking that power. In his current state, Monson couldn't recall why that was so important to his grandfather, just that it was.

Many details like this had come back to him slowly. Learning about one's past might seem scary at first, but as freakish as it sounded, the fact that he couldn't remember much of his was a bit exciting. Memories would come, and it was as if he was reliving his life. It was a funny sensation whenever a memory resurfaced. While it could be disconcerting, it was much better than the gaping void that existed prior to the recovery of a memory.

Monson scanned the books and smiled as he saw that the titles were shelved in alphabetical order. Monson guessed that Brian probably had something to do with this. He seemed like the type who would. A few of them caught his interest with amusing titles or nice-looking covers. Monson pulled a few. He was always looking for something to read, and here was as good a place as any to browse. Most of the books were histories that were militaristic in nature. Some were accounts of modern conflicts: the Persian Gulf Wars, Vietnam, Korea, World Wars I and II, the Civil War—just to name a few. Most, however, were historic accounts of ancient battles. The Roman Empire and its many epic accounts were recorded in multiple volumes. One large series of books seemed to encompass Roman history, from the formation of the Roman Republic to the fall of the Byzantine Empire. Monson was relieved to see that despite the school's obsession with Old Rome, there were many books dedicated to other empires, such as Egypt, Persia, and Syria. Monson idled around the shelves for a bit longer, hoping to find something that might entertain him during his off nights. It was in that moment that something on the back-center bookcase caught his eye.

Lore of the Folk: A Complete Guide to Your Understanding of the Secrets of Coren County read the title. Curious, Monson pulled the book off the shelf and proceeded to examine the cover, which was dominated by a painting of a rock-laced waterfall. It was beautiful, almost as realistic as a photograph. Monson traced his finger along the right side of the picture. He wondered if these falls were actually in the valley or if this was just some artistic license meant to make Coren County appear more interesting than it really was.

Monson flipped open the cover to look for something resembling a dedication or author's note. Instead, he found these handwritten phrases: *For Rose Mary, may you never find this, but if you do, hopefully it helps.*

Monson continued to flip. The book was handwritten and was more like a scrapbook than a published piece. And what about the dedication? Now that was weird.

"Well, you seem a little out of place here, don't you?" Monson asked out loud. "What about this valley could be so interesting that someone would want to write a history of it?"

"Master Grey," a voice split the air from the other room. Monson recognized it as Brian's.

"Yeah, I'm in here, Brian." Monson quickly closed the book. He hesitated for a moment, and without really thinking, he tucked the book under his arm and left the room, closing the door behind him.

Brian was standing behind the counter of the kitchenette holding a tray with an assortment of food.

"I was not aware of your preference, so I brought you a little bit of everything." He set the tray on the counter and offered Monson a couple of different soft drinks. Monson grabbed a can, at the same time placing the book on the stool beside him. He cracked it open and started to drink.

"I don't usually drink a lot of pop," Monson commented, taking a sip of the blue-canned cola. It was a bit sweet, but he found that he liked it. Setting down the soda, Monson picked up a ham and cheese bagel sandwich and bit into it. It was simple but tasty.

"What teenager does not drink soft drinks?" Brian leaned over the plate of food but didn't take any himself. Monson, noticing this, grabbed another sandwich and placed it in front of him. Brian looked startled.

"You look hungry." Monson gestured to the food. "Why don't you join me? Besides, we're probably going to be spending quite a bit of time together, so we might as well be friends."

Brian studied Monson with soft, unassuming eyes. He smiled gently and picked up the sandwich. "Thank you," he said as he took a bite, "but back to the soft drinks; I'm curious. Why do you not drink them? Are you an athlete?"

Monson laughed. "No, I've never played any sports as far as I know. I was homeschooled, so that makes it hard, you know."

"You were homeschooled, were you? Why stop now?" Brian asked, "And in such a dramatic way? Did homeschooling not suit your taste?"

Monson didn't answer but stuffed the rest of the sandwich into his mouth, almost choking as he did so. Finally, he was able to swallow.

"I think I'm going to lie down now," he said, a slight edge to his voice.

"I see." Brian straightened up and gave Monson another one of those little bows. "I will wake you when the time is right. Rest assured knowing I will be here, and thank you for the sandwich."

Monson touched his fingers to his brow in a kind of half-salute and proceeded to his room, closing the doors behind him.

Alone now, he walked across his room and sat on the large window seat that ran the length of the huge window. It was raining outside. A gentle patter of drops stuck to the glass as the remnants drizzled down the length of the window. The sight and sounds were soothing. Monson stared out to the forest that marked the edge of Coren's property. The area stretched on forever, the lush greenery reaching far into the distance. Monson liked the rain, but only if he had a dry spot from which to watch it. The hospital in Seattle often saw rain, and Monson enjoyed watching the downpour from his window, much like he was doing—

Movement in the distance, just in front of the tree line, drew his attention. A single person moved out from the darkness and ran south along the tree line. The figure wore a dark cloak and seemed to blend into the dark forest.

The gloom made it difficult to see. But then the person stopped and turned in Monson's direction. The distance made it impossible for him to be certain, but Monson had the very distinct feeling that he — it was definitely a man in the cloak — was looking straight at him.

"Master Grey, I am going out for a moment. Do you need anything?"

Monson turned reflexively to answer. "Um...no, Brian. I do not. Thanks."

Monson returned his attention to the window, but the figure was gone. Disappeared.

Strange, thought Monson as he searched the tree line. He couldn't have just disappeared? Where did he go?

Monson's question went unanswered, though the most obvious answer was that the man had retreated into the forest. Still....

Monson's attention lingered on the forest for some time. He did not know why, but the disappearance of the cloaked man tugged at something in the back of his mind. Eventually, the rain's steady patter turned his thoughts involuntarily to Brian. He sighed. He had been short with the manservant. Brian didn't know anything about his past —no one did. It wasn't fair for Monson to treat him like he did.

Monson removed himself from the window and flopped onto the bed, stretching his arms and legs, tightening the muscles as much as he could. He winced as he felt the strain of scarred skin that covered a large part of his body.

"One more reminder of what I can't remember." Monson gritted his teeth, determined to finish his stretching.

Monson slid his hands toward the space between his headboard and mattress, hoping to find an edge or lip he could grab. There wasn't one; the headboard seemed to continue all the way down to the floor. Annoyed at being unable to accomplish his stretch, Monson moved his fingers farther down the headboard. He stopped when his hands slid over a strange indention. Monson's fingers lingered. To the touch, it didn't feel like it was a part of the original design; it felt too random and rough. He struggled, curious why there would be such distinct marks on a well-crafted hardwood bed frame.

Could the bed be from a used furniture store? Monson stifled a laugh but realized that he didn't need to; he was the only one privy to the thought. What a ridiculous thought. There was no way that could be. All the same, Monson did his best to envision Dean Dayton shopping at a Liquidation World or Goodwill. The thought made Monson giggle. He continued running his fingers over the indentations. He realized that the markings ran at least part of the length of the bottom portion of the bed, were finely cut, despite their out-of-place location, and fairly deep.

Ahh, screw this, Monson thought, extracting his arm from the space between the bed and the headboard. He slid with a dull thump off the side of the bed and picked up the mattress, intending to tear it off. The mattress was heavier than he had expected. He strained, and with a final thrust, the mattress slid partially to the side and exposed a heart with a set of initials chiseled into the wood.

Monson laughed aloud. How anticlimactic—all that curious excitement for some cheesy declaration of puppy love. Annoyance kicked in. Monson took a closer look at the initials: *G.D.P. & M.P.* He made a mental note to make fun of whoever wrote that and then grabbed the mattress to heave it back into position.

"Heavy little sucker, aren't you?"

Monson struggled for a few moments more and finally shoved the mattress in place. Unfortunately, he wasn't paying attention to his footing. He fell, kicking the frame of the bed just hard enough to move it slightly. He hit the ground with a solid *thump*, and slid lightly across the floor to a stop just as a second *thump* broke the silence.

Monson lay on the ground panting.

Brilliant, Grey, just brilliant. It was then that the sound finally registered. What was that second *thump?*

Monson, crawling, forced his way under the side of his bed to investigate. He pulled out a small metal box.

The container appeared totally unremarkable. Tarnished and faded, probably from many years of use, it appeared to be shut tightly.

Annoyed, Monson almost gave the small tin a toss. Honestly, why on earth would this be wedged up behind his bed? He couldn't think of anything more stupid. There was no reason for that to be there unless... someone was trying to hide it. Monson paused and looked at the container. This could be something private and important forgotten by the previous owner.

Then again, he or she did leave it. In which case, it couldn't be that important, especially in a place that appeared to be more for convenience than hiding.

Monson fingered the lid of the box. There couldn't be any harm in just looking, could there? Monson decided not, and slowly wedged the lid off of the container.

Paper and envelopes of every shape, size, and color came spilling out, along with accumulated filth. How long had this thing been in here to have this much dust? A sweet scent permeated the air as remains of a perfume washed over him. A girl wrote these. The handwriting, or what could be seen of it, was small and full of loops too feminine to be a boy's. Monson grabbed one of the pages and opened it. He read the title, written in the same embellished handwriting.

The Queen's Chronicle - Conquering the Ridge by M.P.
She followed a path of her own choosing.
One that scaled the height of her own mountain.
A journey started with a voice, which said:
Come, find your other self.

Long was the quest along the winding trail
Deep were the rivers she traversed
Dark were the woods she explored.
Difficult were the keepers who confounded her.

She withstood with the allure of the natural man
She calmed the core of the enlightened soul
She found the secret of the translated other self
Only to lose herself to the worlds.

The path, the war, still wages on.

Red for passion and anger's heat
Blue for docile souls that are ever upbeat
Yellow for freedom; the expressive self
Green for the solid being; the foundation for all else.

A woman followed a path of her own choosing
One that scaled the height of her own mountain
She started her journey with a single step
And found the other's gate enigma at its peak.

Monson stopped reading, attempting to understand. *What in the world is this?* He picked up some more of the papers; it went on for at least two more pages. If this was a love letter, it didn't seem like a very good one. What happened to "How do I love thee? Let me count the ways"?

As Monson replaced the poem and properly stacked the mismatched groups of paper, a picture caught his eye. He pulled it out of the stack. It was a painting—an amazing one.

Vibrant colors of a sunset highlighted a castle like no other. Large, with an airy, open architecture, the fortress sat on a pair of cumulus clouds suspended hundreds, maybe thousands of feet in the air. In the distance, four peaks encircled a lush, green valley. The colors were bold and beautiful. Monson couldn't take his eyes off of it. He smiled as he pictured in great detail a place like this castle on a cloud. Monson flipped the picture over to see if there was a signature. He found the same insignia as on the poem, *M.P.* He made a mental note: Figure out who M.P. was.

Monson grabbed the container and lid and replaced the papers, including the poem, but kept the picture out. He returned the tin to under his bed. He lay down, looking at the picture and recounting the events of the day. Day... bah! It wasn't even three o'clock yet! He sighed, feeling the tiredness creep through him. Between almost being clubbed by Artorius, knocking the crap out of one of the prettiest girls Monson had ever seen, the weird gray stone hanging around his neck, oh, and let's not forget the weird out-of-body experience or whatever that was when Dean Dayton called his name, he felt that he had experienced enough for one day. He hoped this wasn't going to be a daily thing.

CHAPTER 5
NIGHTMARES

IMAGES PLAYED at the edge of his consciousness, creating a webbed but disjointed slideshow. Scenes seemed connected but confused, like a storyboard that had been tipped and jumbled, disjointing the order and twisting the timeline. Suddenly, the screeches of women—some in pain and others in panic—permeated the air as gobs of liquid fire enveloped them, searing their bodies and finally silencing them. Screams in a forgotten language left his mouth, joining the throngs of agonized moans as an eerie silence and pain overtook him. As quickly as it started, it stopped. Blackness threatened to over-come, but then the scene changed, or maybe it just became clear, because the vision of a man wearing a cloak came into focus. He was bathed in red flame, and his step crushed the concrete beneath him while tempestuous winds swished and swirled around him. He walked forward, holding something in his hand that seemed solid but at the same time wavered with pulsing energy. Hatred so intense it almost took a physical form radiated from the cloaked man as he moved closer to where a second man lay panting. The second man seemed defeated; he lay battered, bloody, and bruised. The cloaked man grinned, purpose shining in his movements, and an aura of evil—

pure evil—surrounded him. He moved on, but it seemed to take a long time for him to get close to where the second man lay. It was as if he were fighting an invisible force that impeded his progress. As the second man lay there, repulsion seeped in, emboldening him to move. He did so, but being too weak, merely stumbled back to the ground. The man with the cloak approached calmly, getting closer and closer. His cruel eyes shone under the dark cloak as finally the shadow of a face could be seen. The embodiment of fear peered out from the darkness of the cloak as a countenance was both lit up and thrown into relief by the light of the object positioned aggressively in his hand. A smile played across cruel lips as he raised his hand to strike—

———

MONSON AWOKE WITH A START, breathing heavily and feeling slightly feverish. The curtains darkened his room, making it impossible to tell the time of day. Monson reached up, placing his hand on his forehead, and felt cold beads of sweat on his brow. How long had he been asleep? It couldn't have been long, but there was no way of telling because of the curtains, and he didn't have a watch with him. Monson noticed a pitcher of water sitting on the bedside cabinet to his left. He stood up, retrieved the pitcher, and poured water into a glass, downing the contents in two great gulps.

And people always wonder why I look so tired, Monson thought wryly. He climbed back into bed and stared at the ceiling. Strange images flashed across his vision as realization hit him. A dream, yet another, that he could barely remember. He closed his eyes, trying to grasp and decipher what he saw.

Pain. Screaming. Distinct. Familiar—damned familiar. Everything is damned familiar! Monson opened his eyes, punching his bed in frustration. He had dreamt of something important, but now he couldn't remember the dream or why it was important. Was it a repressed memory or a piece of the past? *Why? Why couldn't he remember?*

Monson felt like tearing his hair out, if only to give him something else to ponder. This vision or nightmare was different—a new dream from a new avenue of the mind. He felt that, but he didn't know how to latch onto these dreams. He probably never would.

This line of thought made Monson wonder about his past self. A single moment had wiped out the person known as Monson Grey, and now lying on this bed was a shadow of that person, that seemingly fictional being, who wrestled with his own fears and the realities of his life. When he looked in the mirror, he didn't recognize the face looking back at him.

Monson rolled onto his stomach.

What am I left with? Where do I go from here? Will these dreams ever make sense?

Monson paused. *His dreams.*

Monson wondered what his dreams were like before the attack took everything from him. Were there dreams he could remember? Were they full of happy thoughts and silly desires? Did they reflect his heart, his wishes, his humanity?

Humanity?

Monson scowled to himself.

What humanity? What is humanity, even? Does having dreams and ambitions make up your humanity? Or is it something else? Something like...

Fear.

What was there to fear? Monson wasn't sure. But he did know that he had fears: fear of the known, the unknown, the probable, and the possible. He feared death. The idea scared him. But more than death, he had a fear of life—living when he did not know himself. He just had fear.

Monson let out a long yawn, exhaling the air and with it those difficult subjects.

What was with these depressing thoughts? Be thankful you're alive. A lot of people aren't. You were spared. You were lucky.

"That's right," Monson said out loud. He looked for something else to occupy the time.

Maybe I'll do some reading.

After a moment or two of looking, Monson found his backpack right inside the door to his room. He assumed that Brian put it there, as he couldn't remember doing it himself.

In his current state of memory loss, the only thing Monson could depend on was Molly. She had been there for him, rarely leaving his side in those first difficult days. Those had been some of his most trying, the ones right after he awoke from his comatose state. He awoke knowing so little and seeing only strangers in a strange place. Yet Molly was there for him. That was truly a time he would never forget. He remembered the touch of Molly's hand as she asked how he was doing. He remembered the look on her face when he asked, "Who are you?" He remembered her scanning his frame and the rich detail of her tear-filled eyes as she took in his scarred and torn body.

Monson felt the rims of his eyes water.

Tears?

He dabbed at the corners.

Hope for understanding and recovery did come, however. Molly made sure of that. They spoke long into the night, and slowly, painfully, as if he was trying to pull pieces of himself through a mesh net, Monson began to remember; memories flooded back to him. They weren't much, but they were his. He knew it would be a long time until he was back to normal, assuming that he got there at all.

Monson paused at this. *Normal. What is normal?* Monson possessed no concept of the word; the idea remained beyond his reach.

He chuckled as he thought about the whole ordeal. Coren. Baroty Bridge. His grandfather. All of those people. Monson stopped laughing, ashamed of his actions. These were not laughing matters. Monson tended to use humor to deal with stress, which probably wasn't always the best idea, but "go with what works" was his philosophy. Monson adjusted his body, trying to find a more comfortable position.

He felt drained, weak, and tired... always tired. He was so uncomfortable.

He stood up and again headed to the window seat. The cushion was nice and soft, made of an odd, water-smooth material. Monson moved the blackout shade to reveal soft, gloomy gray light, courtesy of storm clouds congregating above Coren Valley. The rain appeared to be gone for the time. It was all the same to him. He leaned against the window, hoping his unpleasant thoughts would drain from him just like the water drops draining from the side of the building.

Suddenly, Monson sat bolt upright, disgust threatening to overcome him. How could he forget something that important? No wonder he was having nightmares! He jumped out of bed and ran to the double doors, throwing them open with gusto. He searched for his luggage, scanning the room. He found the suitcases propped carefully against the opposite wall. Running over to them, he started tearing at them in a frenzy, opening bags and sealed packages alike, taking little notice of the contents. With a sigh of relief, he found it. A dark rag covered a small old wooden frame. It had been wrapped with such care that although it was obvious the frame was old, the dark wood gleamed brilliantly, displaying neither scratch nor blemish.

Sorrow assaulted Monson as he held up a photograph of a smiling man. Gray hair, messy and unkempt, fell into soft, kind eyes that spoke of dignity and experience. Monson smiled, cradling the picture, and feelings of contentment welled up inside. He walked purposefully to his nightstand and placed the framed photograph on the bedside table with tender affection. He took one last look at it before crawling back into bed. So much had happened to him in the last few months, and now he once again found himself in a strange place with strange people. He felt overwhelmed and alone.

I am so sorry, Monson thought as he lay in his bed. *I won't forget again.* As sleep enveloped him, he muffled a simple goodnight to the man in the picture. He knew that he would sleep better this time because his grandpa was watching over him.

BOOM... Boom... Boom!

What is that? Monson groaned sleepily, still under a copious amount of covers. He heard it again.

Boom!

Was it getting louder?

BOOM!

The sound... it felt like... something was here. Right on top of him.

Ahh, crap, Monson thought. He thought he knew what the "boom" was. Monson pushed the comforter off his head and caught a fleeting glimpse of Artorius leaning on the big oak doors. He appeared greatly amused. Before Monson could say anything, he felt a sharp pain in his chest as Casey's high-flying form crumpled into him.

"Time to get up, Scarface!" Casey dug his elbow further into Monson's chest, knocking the wind out of him. "You've slept long enough."

It took Monson a minute to get Casey off and inhale enough air to answer. "What time is it?" Monson tried to rub the tiredness out of his eyes.

"Five thirty. You see, you've gone and spoiled everything now." Casey grinned. "You aren't going to sleep tonight, and you'll be extra-tired for class tomorrow."

"Speaking of which," Monson said, suddenly thinking of something, "when do we find out our course schedules?"

"Tomorrow morning," Casey replied, propping himself up on an elbow next to Monson. "Though four of our classes are already chosen for us." His face soured slightly. "Comes with the territory, I guess."

There was a loud rumble, making all three boys jump. Laughter broke out when Monson's stomach gave another massive grumble.

"Dude," Casey said through a burst of mirth, "when was the last time you ate? You sound like you're dying."

"It's been a couple of days since I've eaten properly," Monson admitted. "I was just too nervous to keep anything down."

"Well, that settles it, doesn't it!" Artorius exclaimed. "We need to find this boy some food."

"It's about that time anyway," Casey agreed, checking his watch, "or you know we wouldn't bother." He grinned deviously, seeing how Monson would react to his banter.

"Really," Monson's eyes narrowed as he caught on. "Hey Case, how's Kylie? As I recall, you have a story to tell us." Then, looking at Artorius, he added, "Well, you have a story to tell ME at least."

Casey blanched and tried to reply but appeared to be at a loss for words.

"Ahhh," Monson crooned mockingly in a high voice, "You're embarrassed. How sweet!"

Casey flushed a deep crimson, and Artorius laughed. Instead of answering, Casey slid off the bed and started to move toward the door. Monson laughed and threw a fist in the air. "It looks like that's one for me, *Cassius.*"

Casey suddenly stopped, as if he was contemplating something, and then said abruptly, "Ah, screw this!" He unexpectedly whipped around and ran, jumping at the last second. Monson watched in horror as Casey sailed toward him. "All right, Hero," Casey yelled through muffled laughter as he landed on top of Monson for at least the third time that day, "let's see what you got!"

CHAPTER 6
RECEPTION

"SO WHERE DOES a brotha go to find some grub 'round here?" Casey inquired in a loud, obnoxious voice. "Arthur, isn't there supposed to be some sort of student store?"

"Don't call me Arthur, Cassius."

"Holy Hannah freaking Montana, you're annoying. Are you gonna answer my flipping question, or am I going to have to beat it out of you?"

Artorius contorted his face in a comical fashion, crossing his eyes and showing Casey a silly smile. Casey tried to fight it, but before long, he busted out in chuckles. They had a good laugh.

"OK, but seriously," Casey wiped a tear from the corner of his eyes, "Grey is scarred and scary. He shouldn't be ghastly and malnourished too. That's just bad form."

"Casey!" Artorius glanced over at Monson as he attempted to whisper. "What did I tell you? You can't say crap like that. Grey might be sensitive."

Monson raised an eyebrow. "Umm... I can hear you, Arthur, and don't worry, I don't mind. Casey's complete lack of tact or anything resembling charm is refreshing."

Casey smiled and bowed. Monson chuckled as his eyes wandered toward the window. The image of a cruel smile from underneath the unnatural blackness of a hood jumped out at him so unexpectedly that he flinched.

He quickly regained his composure, but Casey and Artorius noticed.

"Dude, are you OK? You seem a little jumpy."

Monson looked back at the window. Nothing. He rubbed his eyes and tried to think of something, anything, to tell them. "Well... you see... I was just thinking about these... weird... things on my bed."

Casey yawned. "Now that was an articulate and well-expressed thought."

Monson rolled his eyes. "The bed... there were these weird markings on the bed, and I was just thinking about them. I found them when I was trying to stretch earlier."

They stared at him vacantly.

Monson smiled. "So I stretch! Apparently, scar tissue makes it hard to move. Who knew?"

Artorius scratched at his head. "Grey, what do you mean by weird markings?"

"Well, weird is not exactly the word—more like comical. Here, I'll show you."

Monson pulled back the bed and mattress to show Casey and Artorius the heart and initials.

They both giggled like schoolgirls. Artorius was having a difficult time breathing. "Who seriously does that?"

Casey wasn't any better off. "Did we magically fall into a 1920s flick without me knowing it?"

Artorius shook his head. "Those films were silent; like, there was no sound."

He stared at Casey. "If only."

"Har har har, Arthur," Casey sneered. "Notice no one was laughing?"

They both faced Monson expectantly.

"Don't look at me. I'm just a bystander. Besides, I maintain that neither of you are very funny. So I'm not sure what you're arguing about."

Both Casey and Artorius tried not to smile.

"Now, back to the food problem—"

"I think I can help you with that particular issue, Master Grey."

Brian entered Monson's room carrying three pairs of slacks, button-ups, sweater vests, and shoes. He arranged them at the foot of Monson's bed.

"Boys, if you would be so kind as to line up." Brian gestured to the bed.

The three boys exchanged looks. Casey was the one that spoke. "Yeah... so I don't believe we've actually been formally introduced."

"Cassius Kay and Arthur Paine, yes, I'm well aware of who you are. Now hurry, or Master Grey will be late."

Monson stifled a laugh; the expression on Casey's face was price-less. Accompanied by a significant amount of glaring, Casey did as he was told. The three boys lined up, shoulder to shoulder. Brian grabbed a set of clothes and held them up to the boys, sizing up each of them as he did. He took measurements and appeared pleased with himself.

Casey whispered a little louder than he probably meant to, "I feel like he's taking measurements for my coffin. Grey, are you sure this guy works here?"

Artorius' whisper wasn't subtle at all. "At least you're small and fit into most standard coffins. If he kills me, then I'll probably just be dumped in the woods."

Casey shook his head. "With that fire-bush you call hair, they'd find you too quickly. No, he'd chop off those hairy hobbit feet of yours to make you fit in a smaller box. Serves you right for being so tall."

Artorius raised a hand, placing it over his eyes. "Why I haven't popped you like the zit you are is beyond me."

Casey returned the banter with a rude gesture.

"Well, it appears I was spot-on with your sizes. Now all you need to do is change."

The three boys gawked at him.

"Change?" Monson asked. "Change for what?"

"For your reception, Master Grey. Now you need to hurry, or you're going to be late for the ball."

———

"MR. GATT IS SO GETTING PUNCHED when I see him next," Monson stated as he lingered side-by-side with Casey and Artorius. "Why didn't he say anything about this?"

Artorius bit into a chunk of light, fluffy cake. He relished it before he answered. "He did, Grey, earlier. It's not so bad. At least for the most part, people are ignoring us."

That was certainly true. Not more than two people had said a word to Monson, Casey, or Artorius since the moment they had entered the lavish reception hall. This seemed odd to Monson; this was supposed to be a reception for the new *Horum Vir*, and as far as he knew, *he* was the new *Horum Vir*.

"There's food, so I'm not going to complain." Casey popped a meatball into his mouth. "They must have had a Master Chef's take on this. I'm almost positive the meatballs are Kobe beef."

Monson helped himself to one. It was absolutely *amazing*. OK, so the reception wasn't so bad.

"May I have your attention, please?"

The crowd quieted and turned toward a podium, similar to the one at orientation. Dean Dayton flashed a million-dollar smile. "I want to thank you all for coming tonight and on such short notice. It has been quite the year for...."

Another speech. Monson sighed and let his mind wander. When was this thing going to be over?

"Mr. Grey, yes, yes, Mr. Grey, would you mind coming up?"

Monson froze. What had the Dean just been saying? He really needed to start paying attention.

The beam of a bright spotlight settled upon him, and the only sound came from the uncomfortable throat clearing that seemed to have stricken many of the guests. Not knowing what else to do, Monson walked slowly to the front of the room. Applause followed, trickling in at first, before more of the audience joined in. The hall was roaring by the time he stood at the podium. Dean Dayton clapped as well, an incredibly fake smile affixed to his face. Monson smiled back and tried to look genuine, even as his mind raced.

Why would the Dean call him up here when they were doing such a fine job ignoring him? Monson squared himself behind the podium as the dean wrapped an arm around him. "Smile, Monson, all these people came to see you."

"Why would they come to see—"

"Ladies and gentlemen, I proudly present to you Monson Grey! Monson, why don't you tell us a bit about yourself? Where you come from, where you grew up, what's happened to you in the last few months."

There was more clapping as the dean removed himself from the spotlight. Monson faced the crowd he could not see, his throat going dry. He didn't know what to do. He couldn't remember his past. What was he supposed to say?

The clapping lasted another thirty seconds and then died down in a fairly dramatic fashion, or maybe it just felt that way because of Monson's current predicament. The glare of the spotlight beat down on him. He managed to get out a few words. "Umm... yeah, well, like the dean said, I'm Monson Grey."

Monson froze. His voice failed him, and his palms started to sweat. What the heck was he supposed to talk about? Maybe just some general information.

"I grew up here in Washington, in the central part, near Moses Lake. I was homeschooled... and... I like history."

Monson swallowed hard. That was about all he knew. He didn't know what else to say. Monson attempted to choke out another phrase. "I—I'm... happy to... to be here. Um... thank you."

Monson started to move away from the podium. An arm was around him before he could take more than half a step out. The dean was back at his side. "Thank you, Mr. Grey. Are there any questions for our new *Horum Vir*?"

An outbreak of movement and whispering among the audience made Monson wonder what they were all so worked up about. Monson was able to catch some of the chatter.

"Grey, as in *him*, as in *the* Grey?"

"Ask him what happened."

"Are you insane? No way! You ask him."

A woman's voice carried over the others, who were whispering. "Mr. Grey, yes, Mr. Grey. I'm Carol Williams. Just wanted to ask you a quick question: As the sole survivor of Baroty's Bridge, can you tell us what happened that day?"

Monson suddenly lost his ability to inhale, yet he didn't feel surprised by the question. That is what people really wanted to know. It was probably even the reason for the last-minute reception. It happened only a few months ago, and the investigation was still ongoing. Of course, it was still ongoing; it was the worst attack in American history, and they had no idea who did it.

Monson didn't say anything, or rather, was unable to say anything. It was unnaturally silent in the hall, like the audience was holding its collective breath. Monson looked skyward, only to see shadows. A flicker of movement caught his eye. The shadow—it moved. Monson tried to find the source. No luck; the lights were too bright.

"Good evening, ladies and gentlemen."

Monson looked to his left, hoping to see an ally, someone, anyone who might rescue him from this. Mr. Gatt stood calmly at his side; he was already addressing Ms. Williams.

"Ms. Williams, was it? I hate to be the bearer of bad news, but the

Department of Homeland Security has specifically forbidden Monson from discussing the matter. National security, you understand. Besides, you would not want to put our young *Horum Vir* on the spot like that. It makes it appear that you have some kind of ulterior motive."

Monson had difficulty seeing Ms. Williams, but the note of discomfort in her voice was conspicuous. "Just curious! We're all so interested to get to know him as a representative of our school."

"Oh, well, as you can see, the caterers are passing out gift baskets now. An information packet has been included on Mr. Grey. Now, I am sure you are all dying to come and get to know Mr. Grey better, so we'll move along with the greeting portion of the evening. Please form a line at the base of the stage."

"Wait a moment," Dean Dayton tried to whisper. "Markin, what are you doing? Wait, I still—"

Mr. Gatt ignored the dean and steered Monson to a large stool. The dean stared after them, then, with a flash of anger, stormed off. The lights dimmed, and Monson rubbed at his eyes. He could finally see properly. He did not like what he saw.

There was already a line—a big one. More than twenty people chatted among themselves while Mr. Gatt situated Monson.

"Mr. Gatt, what are you doing?"

Mr. Gatt whispered to him, "Saving you from answering a great deal of invasive questions, which I doubt you want to answer. Now sit."

Monson sat on the stool. The regal but frumpy woman at the head of the line came to him and offered a hand.

"Monson, this is the Duchess of Devonshire. She is a longtime supporter of Coren and responsible for most of the art you see on the campus."

"I also saw your performance at the Knowledge Bowl last year," the Duchess offered. "Marvelous, my dear boy, absolutely marvelous. I was sad to hear that you were part of the tragedy at Baroty's Bridge. How on earth did you ever survive such a horrible—"

"I apologize, Duchess," Mr. Gatt bowed formally, "but Mr. Grey has many people to meet tonight. If you like, I will take your card, and you can contact Mr. Grey for a meeting, his schedule permitting, of course."

The Duchess shot Mr. Gatt a murderous stare. Monson was quite glad not to be on the receiving end of that. But the Duchess had enough tact not to make a scene; she exited quietly, without leaving her card.

"One down, Mr. Grey."

Monson tilted his head back to look at Mr. Gatt. "One down?"

Mr. Gatt smiled. "Yes, and probably one hundred or so to go."

Monson swore under his breath.

Mr. Gatt's grin grew wider. "My sentiments exactly."

Monson raised an eyebrow. "I thought you said that swearing was the product of a deranged mind, or something."

Mr. Gatt patted Monson on the shoulder. "Close enough, but in this case, I am willing to make an exception. These people make me want to swear. Endure. We will accomplish this rather daunting task together. Now, the next guest is the head of Apple..."

Monson sat up a little straighter. It was going to be a long night.

———

"IF I EVER HAVE TO DO THAT again, I am simply going to put a bullet in my head."

It was close to midnight, and Casey, Artorius, and Monson were walking with Mr. Gatt through the massive reception hall.

"You did well." Mr. Gatt navigated the hall at a leisurely pace, but it was obvious he was tired, and with good reason. Mr. Gatt had spent most of the night helping Monson dodge any sort of personal questions, and doing so with such poise and charm that it was impossible to take offense. The man had obviously played this sort of political game before.

Monson shot a skeptical expression at Mr. Gatt. "I did well? I didn't do anything. You were the one insulting people in a brutally polite manner. You gonna tell me what all that was about?"

"Dude, I thought you were smart." Casey showed Monson one of the many well-known Internet search engines on his phone. "You'd probably guess if you took half a second to think about it."

Monson looked at the most commonly searched term of the hour, day, week, and even month. "Baroty's Bridge" lit up brightly for all eyes to see.

There were millions of searches on that term within the last hour alone.

"It must be a slow news week," Monson commented. "Baroty's Bridge happened months ago."

Casey asked incredulously, "Dude, have you been living in a box? Look at the headlines."

He pulled up a news feed search highlighting every story, article, or blog mentioning Baroty's Bridge. He put his phone up to Monson's face as they reached the doors leading outside, where they were greeted with a blast of surprisingly cool air. Monson grabbed Casey's phone and scanned the most popular results. There were millions of hits. Apparently, Baroty's Bridge was a hot topic. If that was the case, why was everyone making such a ruckus about him?

"Speculation," Casey answered, as if he were reading Monson's thoughts.

Monson stopped dead in his tracks. Mr. Gatt gave Casey a reproving look. "Cassius, must we speak of such—"

Monson cut in. "What do you mean, speculation? Casey?"

Mr. Gatt and Casey looked at each other. Casey answered hesitantly, "Monson, no one has any idea what happened at Baroty's Bridge. If you were to read all these stories, blogs, and newsreels, the only thing you'd get is frustrated. There has been no new information in months as to what left everyone on the bridge—all three hundred people—dead. All except you."

Monson's breathing became heavy, and inevitably his thoughts turned to Molly. No wonder she didn't tell him about this.

"Guys," Artorius said, oblivious to the seriousness of the conversation. "Is it just me, or is it really dark out here? I mean, like, zombie apocalypse dark."

Casey snickered, and he launched into baby talk. "Ahh, Arthur, you don't have to be scared of the dark. Cassius will protect you."

His voice switched back to normal. "Oh, and as for the inevitable zombie apocalypse, if you'd just read that book I gave you, you'd be totally prepared."

Artorius scowled. "Please, I could have gotten better zombie protection..."

His voice drifted off. He seemed to be listening to something.

Casey laughed. "Sure, Arthur—"

Mr. Gatt interrupted this time. "No, Cassius, I hear something— Monson, look out!"

Monson looked up just in time to see a flash of bright light and a massive dark object hurling toward him.

CHAPTER 7
TARIS GREEN

"GOOD MORNING, MY DEAR HERO."

Monson awoke from a very nice dream just in time to see a blurred figure pull open the curtains. The light was not welcome. "And how do we fare this fine morning, Master Grey?"

"You mean besides my brush with death?"

Brian's figure slowly became visible. "Yes, of course."

Monson shrugged. "Besides the near-death experience, I'm just fine. Thanks for asking."

"It concerns me that you can be so nonchalant about a giant statue almost crushing you to death."

Monson thought back to the night before. Casey had been the one who sprang into action. The huge gargoyle crashed right where Monson had been standing, and it had been Casey who pulled him out of the way at the last moment. An at-the-buzzer save is a bit clichéd, but Monson would always take that over an unexpected loss. Mr. Gatt freaked out, of course, and immediately took Monson back to his room before summoning Coren's entire on-call medical staff. It was well after 2 a.m. before Monson finally convinced Mr. Gatt and the doctors that he was fine. Surprisingly enough, Monson slept like a baby after that.

Monson shrugged at Brian's comment. "Did you see Baroty's Bridge? A giant falling statue is like a walk in the park."

Brian pulled at the covers, apparently unconvinced. "I'll take your word for it, but know that I have my eye on you. Now, how would you like to take your breakfast?"

Monson cocked an eyebrow. "You lost me there, Bri-guy. How do most people take their breakfast? With a fork, or spoon I suppose, depending on what you're serving."

Brian laughed. For some reason, he seemed to find Monson very funny; it annoyed Monson. "What I mean, Hero, is that unlike most people here, you have a choice. If you prefer, you can take your breakfast with your classmates, or I can have it prepared and brought up here where you can breakfast in peace."

Monson meant to answer Brian's inquiry but was saved the trouble by a knock at the door.

"I'll get it," Monson said quickly before Brian could respond. He moved briskly out from behind the wet bar toward the great oak door, ignoring Brian's objections. Monson gave Brian a look over his shoulder; Brian just smiled and shook his head.

"Whaaaaatz up!" Casey bellowed, strolling into the apartment even before Monson could finish opening the door. Artorius followed. "Aren't you ready yet? We gots places to go, *Hero*. The clock waits for no one. Move it, already!"

"And morning to you, Casey."

"What's going on, Grey?" asked Artorius with a quick smile. "How you doing, you know, after yesterday—well, you know."

"I'll live, I think," Monson winked. "It's not my first rodeo in the near-death experience category."

Artorius smiled but looked unsure.

"Well, boys," interrupted Brian. "It would be prudent for you all to be off for breakfast. You do not want to be late for your first lessons. Do any of you know the way to the GM?"

They glanced at one another and shook their heads vigorously. "Well then, let me acquire a school map and I will show you."

Moments later, the boys found themselves in a sea of people. As Casey went into a full-out rant about football and something called the "power I," Monson was left to observe his fellow students. This was his first time around the entire student body, and he found the experience distasteful. Monson could already see cliques developing among the students, and for some reason, this bothered him. Maybe it was because he suspected he had never been part of a group or crowd and was jealous. He doubted anything would change; he couldn't see himself inducted into the cool kids' clique anytime soon.

Monson looked back over his shoulder at the place that would be his home for at least the next year. He felt distaste rise up again. Looming in the distance, the student dormitory, affectionately called "The Barracks" by the student body, had two wings for males and females and eight floors shared by grades nine through twelve. The Elite quarters, which housed private tutors and their pupils to make tutoring sessions more productive, were on another part of campus.

In The Barracks, male and female students lived in the same building separated by a variety of "safety" precautions, including cameras and elaborate door locks. There were certain times when the electronic measures were taken down, and the students could explore each other's living spaces, but these were closely supervised. All students shared a ridiculously large, two-story common room that was adjacent to and continued underneath the Atrium. Nicknamed "The Jive," the room boasted pool tables, Ping-Pong tables, vending machines, a couple of large TVs, and assorted other means of entertainment. The washing machines and dryers were there as well, though most of the students opted for the Executive Service, or "Ex Service," which provided a staff to handle things like laundry and cleaning. It was a neat place to live for *most* people.

"Excuse me."

A sweet voice caused Monson to almost jump out of his skin. Wrapped up in his own thoughts, he now realized that not only were Artorius and Casey nowhere to be seen, but he stood in the midst of a group of very pretty upperclassman girls. A particularly cute girl with curly strawberry-blonde hair stood in front of him, smiling. He studied her, not sure what to say, and in an attempt to smile, barely managed a grimace. He heard murmuring behind him but ignored it, focusing on the girl.

Her appearance was abrupt and regal, yet demure somehow; quite the contradiction. Her curly hair obscured a portion of her face, which added a little mystery. She was altogether striking.

"I am so sorry," said Monson, addressing the redhead. "I didn't mean to intrude."

The girl did not answer right away, instead studying him curiously with a strange look on her face. "Don't I know you from somewhere?"

"No...I don't think so." Monson took a few breaths to steady himself; the stares of the girl's companions were getting to him. "And if you're trying to pick me up, you don't need to go any further. You had me at hello."

The girl giggled. "But I didn't say hello."

Monson answered without thinking. "You *would* have had me at hello?"

He groaned to himself; did he really just say that?

"It appears that our new Hero has a sense of humor," the girl mused. Her gaze lingered on Monson; her expression was slightly mischievous. Monson was not quite sure what to do at this point. People like her didn't look people like him in the eyes. What was wrong with this girl?

Monson gazed at her. She smiled again. It was soft and inviting. This girl...there was something different about her. He didn't know what to make of it.

"I'm Monson." Monson put forth his hand, trying to sound confident. "How did you know that I'm the new *Horum Vir*?"

"Alas, that is a long story," confessed the redhead. "It actually took me a second to recognize you. I'm sorry about that."

Then, without warning, she curtsied.

Monson just stood, baffled. The girls in the circle laughed again. Monson bowed awkwardly. It seemed like the best idea at the time.

"You still haven't answered my question," Monson peered at her with an analytical eye.

"You're right." Her smile was becoming wider by the second. He raised an eyebrow. Laughing slightly at his reaction, she winked and said, "Let's just say you and I go way back." She gave him a little wink.

Gasps and muttering broke out from the surrounding crowd; Monson had to raise his voice to be heard.

"I didn't catch your name."

"Taris." Her voice, in contrast, was almost a whisper; nonetheless, he could hear every syllable. Every inflection. He could hear her perfectly. "Taris Green."

"Yo, Monson," bellowed a voice from a ways off.

Monson turned from Taris to see Casey and Artorius staring at him, looks of awe comically contorting their faces. Monson laughed and turned back to the redhead.

"I'd better go." He gestured towards his friends.

"Yeah, you're right," she replied. "Maybe I'll see you around, pretty boy."

"Maybe." He smiled at her again. "But only if you're lucky."

Without another word, he turned around and walked smoothly towards the still-gawking Casey and Artorius while thoughts bounced around his head like crackling popcorn.

If you're lucky? What's up with that stupid comment? Who talks like that?

Monson neared Artorius and Casey.

"Has the world gone mad?" asked Artorius, placing his hand over his eyes and squinting into the distance. "How is it that we find you in the company of Taris Green?"

"Is that bad?" said Monson, awakening from his internal monologue.

"No, it's amazing," said Casey, who looked just as bewildered as Artorius. "She's like one of the hottest girls…," he struggled to find the word, "ever. And she's like totally famous."

"She seemed really nice," said Monson tentatively. "Do you guys know her?"

"We've met," said Casey excitedly, "but we've never had what I'd call an extensive conversation. I had a backstage pass to a concert last year." His eyes faded as if he were losing the ability to focus. "There's an outdoor amphitheater called the Gorge in Eastern Washington. She performed there. I met her then."

"I wouldn't call *our* conversation extensive," replied Monson. "We just introduced ourselves. It wasn't a big deal. Though I must say that it was kinda weird when she knew who I was."

"She knew who you were?" inquired Casey. "That is weird. What did she say?"

"Nothing, really," shrugged Monson, "but she called me Hero. Though I guess she could have known that fact any number of ways. Don't know, really; she was a little vague on the details."

"The plot thickens," commented Casey, rubbing his face. He looked thoughtful but quickly switched to confusion. "You certainly are full of surprises, Mr. Grey."

Artorius swore. "I can't believe you were talking to Taris Green! I know people who've been here for two years who haven't even seen her. She's usually on tour."

Monson laughed; the opportunity was too good to pass up: "Yeah, I think she was kind of flirting with me."

Both Artorius and Casey gasped. They stared at him in total and utter disbelief. Monson tried not to laugh.

"Come on," Artorius finally said. "We can ponder the enigma of Monson's popularity later. I'm starving."

He started to move away but stopped suddenly, a pained look on his face. "I can't believe you were *talking* to Taris. Freaking. Green. Bastard!"

Monson and Casey laughed and started walking, heading away from the group of chattering girls. Monson glanced over his shoulder as their pace started to pick up. To his surprise, he wasn't the only one.

Taris?

"Interesting," thought Monson, and then twisting back towards his friends, he pushed the encounter from his mind.

————

"SO THAT'S what it looks like in the light," commented Monson.

Casey rubbed at his chin. "Yeah…are you sure you want to walk near that thing again?"

"It's either that or just stare at it and hope we get nourishment through some sort of osmosis."

Casey nodded. "OK, but make sure that you walk a bit ahead of us."

Monson glowered. "You're too kind."

The boys stood at an archway that marked the entrance to a massive garden and an even larger building that stood out like a mountain behind it. It took Monson a second, but he recognized it. The reception the night before took place in this building. It looked much different to him in the daylight. It helped that he wasn't currently close to dying. The gardens were amazing. Flowers of every kind were divided into neat rows as if guarding the stone pathway and gave off an intoxicating scent. The stone paths and flowers surrounded grassy knolls where willow, oak, cherry, and even pine trees grew, providing both conversation and congregation points. As if this wasn't enough,

Monson thought he also saw the beginnings of a brush maze on the east side of the building.

Monson looked a short distance off to where he was almost crushed by the falling gargoyle statue. The only hint of the encounter was some broken tiles and concrete, which a group of workers had quartered off and were cleaning. Pretty amazing, considering it happened only the night before.

"The Halls," offered Artorius, sounding like he was guiding a group of over-eager tourists. "Though it's almost never called that."

Even Casey looked surprised at this revelation and inquired, "What do you mean by that, Arthur?"

"Don't call me Arthur!"

Casey rolled his eyes but didn't comment. Artorius glared at him but continued with his narration. "Anyway, many of the students call it 'The GM' or 'The Dungeon.'"

"The GM and Dungeon, huh?" Monson chuckled. "What's with all the nicknames? People at this school have too much time on their hands. OK…now I have to ask. Why do they call it that?"

Casey laughed, and even Artorius smiled.

"The GM stands for the Green Mile, after the movie," said Artorius. "Apparently all the disciplinary offices are on the upper floors. You know, detentions — that sort of thing. The expulsion rate here has created 'The Green Mile' effect: If you get sent to the office at the very end of the hall, you don't have much chance of coming out still a student." He stopped, his gaze finding its way to the upper region of the massive building.

"You're right, Grey." Artorius turned to look at Monson. "People do have too much time on their hands. Anyway, the Dungeon nickname has to do with a prank that kids pulled on a freshman a few years ago. Something to do with underground tunnels and a dead body or something."

"Craziness," said Monson idly. He paused as the meaning of what Artorius said hit him. "Wait—did you say dead body?"

His question, however, fell upon deaf ears. At that exact moment, a large group of girls walked by giggling and eyeing the trio. Many of them looked Monson up and down. He thought he heard Taris' name whispered as they passed.

"For someone with no game and the face of a leper, you're awfully popular with the ladies," declared Casey, as if he was saying something both witty and profound.

Monson went red at his words. "Shut up, Casey."

"How do they do that little hip shake thing?" exclaimed Artorius, his gaze following the group of chattering females. His head swayed back and forth with the rhythmic jive of one of the passing ladies. A sober look on his face made him look very comical.

Monson laughed at his expression. But he also wanted him to finish. "Artorius, focus, you were in the middle of a story."

"I was?"

"Yeah, I'm pretty sure I just asked you a ques—"

"Good morning, boys."

All three boys whipped around to see Mr. Gatt dressed in a crisp three-piece suit and standing in a semi-posed position, as if he wanted their approval.

"Looking sharp, Mr. G," said Casey, looking critically at Mr. Gatt.

"Ahh, Cassius, your approval is most heartwarming."

Mr. Gatt eyed Monson. "And how are you this morning after your encounter?"

Monson waved it off. "I'm fine. Accidents happen. Like I said last night. I didn't get hurt, so don't worry," he said this more brusquely than he intended. Luckily, Mr. Gatt got the hint and didn't say any more.

Mr. Gatt gestured to them. "Come boys, walk with me."

Monson, Artorius, and Casey gave each other the merest of half-glances and then fell into step with Mr. Gatt, who was already bounding towards The Halls with surprising briskness.

"Mr. Gatt," said Monson, wanting to make amends for his shortness. "I was wondering, what do you teach here? Like...what's your subject?"

Mr. Gatt gave him a quick glance but responded very casually. "Why do you ask, Hero?"

"Just curious, I guess," Monson hoped he sounded offhand.

"Well," said Mr. Gatt evenly, "if you must know, I teach an experimental history course." He smiled and added, "With the occasional P.E. courses mixed in for fun. You could say that I'm a dabbler in that field."

Casey interjected, looking perplexed. "Experimental history? What the—" Casey stopped short and quickly looked at Mr. Gatt's knowing expression. "I mean, what does that mean? What can be experimental about a history course?"

Mr. Gatt smiled in a satisfied manner. "My history classes are both investigative and analytical in nature, not mere fact-finding. The students in my classes study legends, folktales, and other mysteries, and look at the different factors that might have gone into both their formulation and perpetuation." He paused, looking thoughtful, then continued. "For example, King Arthur. Who was he and how did he acquire his reputation?"

Artorius gave Casey a sharp look, as if to say, "*See*, I told you he existed!"

Casey ignored Artorius. "I don't get it. Why take the time? I mean really, who cares?"

"You should, my dear boy. It is not necessarily important to know just the facts or details of his life, his favorite foods, or things of that nature. What's important is to examine the traditional points of view concerning him and the sources of those points of view. This helps us build both analytical and critical thinking skills. Once acquired, these skills will allow us to observe with limited bias, thus helping us to form conclusions based on observable fact instead of relying on preconceived notions. Which, I hope I do not have to tell you, is one of the greatest skills one can possess."

"If you say so," conceded Casey.

"Sounds interesting," said Monson sincerely. "Are freshmen allowed to take this class, or is it upper division only?"

Mr. Gatt smiled, surprised but pleased, while both Casey and Artorius stared in disbelief.

"I suppose you will find out soon enough." Monson could tell that Mr. Gatt was trying very hard to hide his amusement. "Freshman students have a six-period day. Four of your subjects are chosen for you: English, Math, Social Science, and Physical Science. You are allowed to pick two subjects on your own. I do not usually let freshman students into my history classes, but if the three of you really want in, I'm willing to make an exception."

"I'm in," Monson almost shouted, without even thinking about it. He liked Mr. Gatt, and it would be good to have one teacher he already knew.

"Wonderful," said Mr. Gatt, beaming. "I must confess, I thought even before I met you that I would probably be seeing you in my class."

Monson wasn't sure exactly what to say to this, so he said nothing.

"The Knowledge Bowl is an academic competition, a large part of which focuses on history," Mr. Gatt said. "Only someone who studied very diligently could have won that competition. In turn, only someone that enjoys history would read so much about it. So naturally, I thought I might see the new Hero in my class."

Monson nodded. "Fair enough."

The group reached the first set of doors of the Halls and passed through, Monson holding the door for the others. At the second set of doors, Mr. Gatt stepped forward and grabbed the door handle to let Casey, Artorius, and Monson pass in front of him. "Ouch!" Artorius yelled as he bumped into Casey. A stream of swear words came spilling out as he doubled over. He angrily mouthed through gritted teeth, "Case, what's the deal?"

No answer came.

Monson leaned forward to see around Artorius. "Casey, what's the hold—" He never finished the sentence because one look was all Monson needed to know why Casey stopped.

Casey stood eye-to-eye with a pretty upperclassman girl Monson instantly recognized. Curly blonde hair pulled into a half-ponytail partially hid bluish-green eyes that sparkled behind slightly shaded sunglasses. Kylie Coremack stood in front of Cassius Kay as a deer stands staring into oncoming traffic. Emotions ranging from regret and pain to indignation and outright disdain played across her perfect face. Casey's eyes narrowed and his jaw clenched as he took a step back, gesturing to Kylie to move first. He looked away, avoiding eye contact with her. She moved slowly, not taking her eyes off his, and her gaze softened bit by bit. Casey simply stood unmoving, face averted as if he had suddenly turned to stone. Kylie's friends curiously watched the silent exchange.

Monson felt like saying something, but with no knowledge of their past, decided against it. It would probably just exacerbate an already tense situation. Finally, as if awakening from a trance, Kylie took notice of her surroundings. She realized that about a dozen people were watching their drama. This did not please her.

The understanding brought about an abrupt change in her demeanor. The condescending spitfire Monson had experienced in full force the day before flared back to life. Her eyes went from soft and tender to steely and cold.

Monson assumed Kylie meant to sweep past Casey, a look of maddening superiority re-fixed to her delicate features. Her presumed plans went awry, however. Still paying close attention to Casey but not to her footing, Kylie stumbled, causing the heel of her pump to break off.

Casey was the only one close enough to help, and everyone there knew it. A moment of hesitation, then, quick as a cat, he stepped forward and caught Kylie by the waist, inches from the floor. Kylie Coremack was not a heavy girl by any means. Nonetheless, it was a feat for little Casey to scoop the girl up in a flash and raise her to her feet.

Monson gaped at him. There was no way that was normal. The strength and speed exhibited by Casey were truly unexpected, amazing…unnatural. Can people really move that fast?

What really caught Monson's attention even more than Casey's unexpected physicality was Casey's gentle handling of the now thoroughly embarrassed girl. Fingers filled with tenderness contradicted the scornful tone he used when he spoke of her the previous day. There was an obvious story here — a complicated one.

"You may want to be more careful," Casey whispered. His voice was quiet and almost kind. He watched Kylie right herself and check her appearance in the reflection of the windows. "I may not be here next time."

"I didn't ask for your help," snapped Kylie.

"No, I don't suppose you did."

Palpable silence followed as Casey and Kylie stood watching one another before Casey silently turned around and walked to the door, parting the utterly perplexed girls in his way. Kylie just watched him go, her eyes slightly glazed as though she was looking right through him.

CHAPTER 8
COACH ABLE

"WHAT THE HELL was that all about?" Monson said to Artorius in disbelief. After the scene with Kylie, Casey had beelined it to the nearest bathroom and was now letting out a steady stream of curses as he punched everything in sight. The other two left him alone and talked quietly at a distance.

"Those two have a history."

"Yeah, I figured as much." Monson looked towards Casey in the corner. "Do you know what happened?"

Artorius hesitated. "Yes, I do. To a point, at least."

Monson continued to look at him, as if to say, "Well?"

He hesitated again. "I'm not sure...."

Monson stopped him. "You're right. I should talk to Casey about this." He berated himself inwardly. Trust had to be earned, not taken.

Artorius sighed sympathetically. "Don't worry about it. It's not even what you think. You're our friend."

Monson smiled, turning away as something caught in his throat.

Casey's ranting interrupted his thoughts. Monson looked towards him. Maybe he would try the direct approach.

"Yo, Casey, what's up with you and Kylie? Why all the bad blood?"

The bathroom went silent. Monson wondered if he had upset Casey.

"She's evil," echoed Casey's voice from across the bathroom. "Totally and utterly evil. Enough said." With this, Casey went back to his ranting.

Another ten minutes passed before, finally, Casey strode towards them, out of breath and slightly red, but otherwise fine.

"Are we back to normal?" asked Artorius, calmly gazing at Casey. "Do you have it all out of your system?"

"Yeah, I'm good," answered Casey, "though there are still these." He held out a pair of sunglasses that Monson recognized as Kylie's. "When'd you nick those?"

"'Nick'?" Casey's face was slightly malicious, but his tone sounded playful. It was apparent he was quickly getting back to normal, or at least trying.

"Shut up," said Monson.

Casey's laugh sounded a bit forced, but he answered the question. "I caught them before I went for her. Now I just have to figure out what to do with them." He lapsed into silent thought.

"Well," said Monson questioningly, "what are you going to do with them?"

"Don't know, but I'm pretty sure it'll have something to do with a bird thrower and a shotgun."

"Come on," said Artorius, checking his watch. "We'd better hurry or we ain't gonna get no food. And who can think on an empty stomach?"

"I wasn't aware you could think at all, Arthur," said Casey with mock astonishment. "Wow, this certainly is a day of discovery!"

"How many times do I have to tell you? Don't call me Arthur!"

Monson could only laugh as Casey and Artorius lapsed into wild banter. Yet his mind continued to race, mulling over what he witnessed between Kylie and Casey. Casey did not come out and say it, but whatever Kylie did to him, it was more than just a simple parting of the ways. Alas, he needed further information to form a proper conclusion. He would just have to pay attention to Casey over the next few days to see if he could glean more. With that thought, his attention shifted back to Casey and Artorius.

———

THE GM'S mess room was one word: awesome. It was huge and served every kind of food imaginable: bacon, eggs, toast, English muffins, hash browns, and an assortment of other items like fruit and cereal—and that was just the stuff Monson recognized; there were a host of foreign dishes he couldn't even begin to name. The boys got in line.

"This is a bit more like it," said Artorius, looking around. "All that grandeur was beginning to get on my nerves." Monson agreed. The GM just felt more relaxed with its lack of fine décor and elegant artwork. Not that the place was dumpy. Rather, it just felt comfortable.

"Don't get too excited, Arthur," said Casey. "My uncle told me that they have a formal banquet room for dances and crap like that."

"Yeah," conceded Artorius. "But we don't have to worry about that today...and don't call me Arthur," he added as an afterthought.

The line moved quickly as the older students got their food, ate, and then made their way out of the various exits in the cafeteria. Monson assumed these other students were heading to their different first periods. From these observations, something struck Monson.

"When do we get our schedules? I don't remember them saying anything about it."

He looked at Casey and Artorius, even though Artorius was not even close to paying attention, but was searching the hall somewhat desperately.

"Right after breakfast," answered Casey, still playing with Kylie's sunglasses. "It was like Mr. Gatt said, all the freshmen will hang around here, then we'll choose our optional courses and be on our way."

"I don't remember him saying that," Monson replied.

"You were busy being handled by the Dean at your reception," smirked Casey.

"Ahh…"

Their conversation abruptly stopped when they were finally able to retrieve trays and help themselves to food. The food was hearty and expertly cooked. The boys took full advantage of the buffet, heaping their plates and downing their food with gusto. The breakfast was good and uneventful, and before they knew it, their plates were scraped clean. A previously unnoticed sign told them that freshmen were to head towards the main conference room of the GM. Monson and the others did so, excited to see what classes this school had to offer.

The flow of students made the conference room easy to find. Upon their arrival, Monson noticed a young man in a wheelchair having problems getting through the doors. His chair was caught on some-thing. Apparently, Coren had missed the memo on disability-friendly entrances and exits. Monson ran forward and pulled the chair back to free it.

"Let me help you," he said, leaning around so the boy could see him.

"I don't need any help!" snapped the boy angrily. He looked around at the crowd. "I can do it myself!"

Whoa, touchy, thought Monson, taking his hands off the boy's chair. "Sorry, man. I didn't mean to impose or anything."

"Whatever," said the boy sourly.

Monson, Artorius, and Casey slid past the wheelchair and surveyed the room beyond. Rows of cubicles, teachers everywhere, and students meandering aimlessly made it difficult to navigate. Casey got them back on track when he pointed and said, "Over there, fellas."

Above the cubicles was a large sign; the top of it read "Start Here," with a huge arrow pointing to a stripe of tape on the floor. There was already a fairly long line up to the front row of cubicles, where several students were already heavily engaged with Coren staff.

"Here's as good a place as any," said Casey, gesturing to the rapidly growing line of people. An older student who appeared to be directing the freshman traffic stopped them.

"Monson Grey?"

Monson's eyebrows shot up. "That's me."

"Your friends can continue on, but you need to step over to the side," said the boy, pointing at Monson. His tone felt tainted, as if he were trying to hold back how he really felt about the school, Monson, and just about everything else.

"Why?" asked Monson, surprised at the boy's tone.

"All members of the Legion meet with Coach Able before they finalize their schedules," replied the boy, who could hardly control his sneer. He obviously did not care for Monson.

"Thank you very much. You've been very forthcoming and help-ful," said Monson with just a touch of sarcasm. He gave the older boy a small, cocky wink and stepped aside as directed, exaggerating his movements. The older boy noticed this and flashed him an angry look in response. Casey gave him a cheesy smile.

Artorius wasn't aware of the exchange but hung back talking to a couple of girls. Something must have caught his attention, however, as he was now hurrying towards them, apprehension on his face.

"What was that all about?"

"I don't know, but someone has his shorts in a twist," replied Monson calmly. "Jerk."

"Grey!" called a hoarse and dusty voice. "You're up."

A small man at the end of the cubicle was leaning halfway out, calling to Monson. A bit shorter than Monson, he had an emaciated and slightly feverish look to him. His balding head held remnants of brown hair and more than a few wrinkles. His speech, however, coun-teracted his appearance: When he spoke, he didn't sound weak at all.

His voice was loud with a definite air of command. He beckoned Monson to him.

"Don't just stand there," ordered the man. "Come in, this shouldn't take long."

Monson sat down in one of the two chairs now visible within the cubicle. The man took a seat opposite and pulled out a yellow folder from a file cabinet in the corner. He started to flip through it lazily. It was some time before he spoke.

"As a freshman, it's mandatory to take some type of physical education class," said the man, not taking his eyes off the pages. "Members of the Legion live up to a higher standard, however, so while you can pick any of the five physical education classes available, the later periods are generally more intense."

Monson didn't say anything. He wasn't sure what to say.

"I would also suggest that you use one of your elective periods for additional strength—"

"Question," interrupted Monson. He cringed; he didn't mean to be so abrupt. Well, he was already in it. "Point of inquiry: do I *have* to be a part of this Legion that everyone talks about, or is it something that I can just forgo?"

"Of course you have to be a part of it!" The man looked scandalized. "It's part of the terms of your scholarship; people are *expecting* to see you there."

"Looking forward to it," said Monson sarcastically. "OK, so people are expecting to see me. What exactly do I have to do?"

"Nothing really, the *Horum*—I mean, the Diamond—will pretty much take care of us. Best quarterback we've had in years. Our entire offense is designed around him. The running backs are as well...."

Monson's mind began to wander as the man's voice washed over him, going on about how amazing the Legion was and how awesome it was to be involved. Monson's mind wandered to the night before and the gargoyle statue. He had been fortunate that the giant chunk of cement didn't crush Casey and him. That would have been just his luck: survive Baroty's Bridge only to die the first day of school. Stupid.

"Grey! You even listening?"

"Yeah," Monson lied, "of course."

"Then we're agreed?"

"Sure, why not," replied Monson, wishing he knew what he was agreeing to. Knowing his luck, he was going to end up goat herding in the Sahara.

"Excellent, I'll put you down for the sixth-period free weights course," said the man in a tone of smug finality. "Now there's just the matter of your one other free period. I would suggest a conditioning course, as most of the—"

"Actually," interrupted Monson, "I already know what class I want for my fifth period."

"Really," the man answered in annoyance, "and what would that be?"

"Well," said Monson, trying to keep his tone pleasant, "I heard Professor Gatt has an analytical history course. I'd like to take it. He already said it would be OK."

The older man's brow furrowed so much that Monson wondered if his forehead hurt.

"It should be stated," he replied, his answer clearly calculated, "that it'll be very hard for you to get any playing time...being a freshman and all. We've never had a freshman on the Legion, or even a freshman *Horum Vir* for that matter. If you want to get in a game at all this season, you really should take the fifth-period conditioning course."

He said this as if it cost him a great deal.

Monson, slapped by a sudden realization, did not speak for a moment. The coach did not want him in the weight-training course, let alone the conditioning course. The poor man was just trying to do damage control. No wonder.

"Coach Able—that's who you are, I assume; you never did introduce yourself properly. I have very little interest in playing for the Legion. I also happen to know you have very little interest in trying to get me to play for the Legion," said Monson, a second realization coming to him. "In fact, you're still bothered about how I got into the school in the first place. That I can't help, but let me assure you that I have no intention of messing with your football team. So in the interest of time, let's drop the pretense that you really want me there."

Monson shot him a thin smile that almost instantly turned into a grimace. Why did he always do that? He really needed to replace the filter between his mouth and brain. To Monson's utter astonishment, Coach Able burst out laughing.

"I'd heard you were one who got straight to the point, but I never expected this." He adjusted himself in the seat, becoming noticeably more relaxed. "I'm glad that you and I are on the same page, Grey. It's good to know that even though you aren't an athlete, that brain of yours is at least half as good as everyone is saying."

"I'm trying to figure out if that was a compliment or an insult," replied Monson. "I'm leaning towards insult."

"Now, it's important that you still show up," said Coach Able, as if he suddenly remembered something. "We'll have to find something on this team for you to do." He rubbed his hands together, apparently thinking. "We'll figure out something...maybe kicking...yes, kicking might work."

"Coach Able, maybe I missed something. Why exactly do you have to find something for me to do on the team?" Monson's voice reflected his confusion.

Coach Able narrowed his eyes and looked at Monson suspiciously. Unsure of what to do, Monson waited for Coach Able to speak.

"Grey, when you won this scholarship, did you read *any* of the information that was sent your way?"

Why did people keep asking him that?

"Of course I did," said Monson with indignation. "But it's not like I went through it with a fine-tooth comb! Besides, as you can see by my glowing countenance, I was slightly preoccupied."

Unbelievable as it was, Coach Able had enough tact not to inquire further. He just stared at Monson, and his gaze softened. "Your scholarship is one of the most highly publicized..." he struggled to find the word, "things out there. First game of the year, people aren't going to come just because of our kicking defense, our unstoppable halfbacks, and our amazing quarterback. They'll come because of *you*. You're the first freshman in history to win the *Horum Vir* all-inclusive scholarship, and almost nothing is known about you. People want to know who you are, so they'll be looking for you. I need you to show up or we'll receive a lot of bad publicity."

"Now isn't that interesting," Monson replied thoughtfully. "So what you're saying is that you *need* me, and you want *me* to do you a favor. Isn't that interesting?"

"Grey, what is it you're concocting in that little head of yours?"

"Coach Able, I think you and I are in a place to help each other. Do you have a minute?"

CHAPTER 9
FLIRTING WITH TROUBLE

THIRTY MINUTES LATER, with schedules in hand, Artorius and Monson tried to catch up with their shorter companion.

"So your session with Coach Able started out pretty rocky, huh?" asked Casey.

Monson answered with a self-satisfied smile. "Yeah, it did. How did you know?"

"I was listening to the first half of your conversation but had to leave partway through. I saw him afterward, and he had a huge smile on his face. Things obviously turned for the better. What'd you do? Give him a lap dance?"

"Ahh, Casey, you're so witty I can hardly stand it." Monson did his best to sound calm. It was costing him a great deal. "It was OK. He just wanted to know what I was planning on doing in this unique position of mine."

"What *are* you planning on doing?" Artorius finally fell into step beside his two friends. "Are you even planning on playing on the Legion?"

"No."

"I sense this is a good thing." Casey threw his arm across his body, stretching his back. "But I still don't understand why you aren't pissed. I mean, he made it pretty clear that, basically, you aren't welcome in the Legion—shoot, welcome at Coren for that matter."

"Don't forget that he told me I have to play nice with the media like some sort of performing monkey."

"Like I said—you're OK with that?"

"Of course not, but I got what I needed out of the deal."

Silence, in which Monson tried really hard not to laugh.

Artorius stopped directly in front of Monson. "Well? Are you going to tell us what happened or not?"

"Oh, you want to know what we *said*," responded Monson playfully, a huge smile stretching the width of his face. "I told Coach Able that I wouldn't try to claim my position on the team and would do my P.R. dance if he'd give you two a real tryout. So I hope you two goofballs are as good as you think you are, because if you screw this up, I'll have to kick you both in the teeth."

With that, Monson strolled past his two friends, their shock chiseled on their faces. When they finally snapped out of their reverie, Monson was halfway down the hall. "OK, spit it out!" Casey caught Monson's arm as they rounded a corner. "How on Odin's green earth did you pull that off?"

"Do you really think so?" Monson feigned ignorance. "Because I'm pretty sure that the earth is covered mostly with water, which—and I could be wrong—is more of a blue color, but—"

"Monson!" shouted Artorius and Casey exasperatedly. "Out with it already!"

"OK, OK. Keep your pants on," said Monson, finally. "It really wasn't that hard. He wanted something from me but had no real leverage to get me to do it. So I told him that if he wants me to play nice, then I want something in return. This was the arrangement that we came to: you guys get a special tryout, and I do what he asks. Simple."

"That was ballsy," said Casey with a mix of awe and horror. "Do you know what that man could do to you?"

"Give me the same ridiculous haircut that he has?"

"Stop joking around, this is serious."

"Jiminy Christmas," Monson put up his hands in frustration. "You guys need to chill. If I explain, will you dial it down a notch?"

They both nodded.

"I'm here on an academic scholarship, *not* a sports scholarship. I have zero interest in playing football. As a matter of fact, I probably couldn't even if I wanted to. So, if Coren wants me to do them favors, then they're going to do it my way."

"Your way," interjected Casey. "What does that mean? What are you actually going to do?"

"What am I going to do?" Monson laughed. "That's easy. I'm going to go to practice and watch you guys do your thing, drink some sports drinks, and see if I can get the tape girl to flirt with me. When the media shows up, I will talk the talk, walk the walk, and dance on my head if need be. In return, you guys get the chance to run with the big boys. I hope you don't disappoint me."

Both Casey and Artorius continued to look at him, dumbfounded. Casey's face stretched into a grin. "Well, Artorius, it looks like something good has finally come from your stupidity. If you hadn't mistook Grey for me, we might have never met him."

Artorius nodded in agreement. "Yeah, we were pretty lucky on that one. I swear I thought it was you. He even looked like he was wearing the same thing."

"Strange but fortunate," said Monson, glancing over his shoulder. "Though you must have been really out of it, Artorius. How you could have mistaken me for Casey is beyond me."

Artorius just shrugged. "Who knows? I really wasn't feeling like myself yesterday."

Casey gave him a knowing look. "You were probably just nervous. I didn't sleep at all the entire week leading up to orientation, and my uncle was almost unbearable. I almost stabbed myself in the ears just so I wouldn't have to listen to him."

"Ditto," said Monson. "Molly was driving me nuts."

"I suppose you're right," said Artorius. He still looked unsure but satisfied. He started shifting his gaze from side to side with concerned contemplation. "I don't think this is right, guys. Are you sure this is the correct corridor?"

"It has to be," said Casey, pulling out a small map of The GM. "It has to be; you see we started here...."

Monson let his attention slip as Casey and Artorius tried to figure out where they were. He allowed himself a selfish moment, not being able to help feeling pleased with himself. He found that his confrontation with Coach Able left him with the feeling of invincibility; like no matter what he did, he would come out victorious. Monson knew that it was not a huge victory, that Coach Able was probably getting the better end of their little deal. However, Monson's successes in the past couple of months felt few and far between. He needed this. Besides, it is not very often you have the opportunity to totally disregard a teacher's power trip and turn it to your favor. He had also earned Casey and Artorius' undying loyalty and respect, which was also a good thing.

Casey and Artorius finally figured out the correct route, and they were off again. It was terribly confusing. Just the sheer size of The GM with its maze-like corridors was enough to make even the older students—let alone newbies like them—lose their way occasionally. They got lost again and decided to ask someone.

A small group of upperclass boys were lounging on and around a large circular table next to the entrance of one of the many rooms in The GM. Monson counted four of them. A set of twin brothers, who looked like they may have come from India, leaned against the wall. A large round-faced boy with more chins than hands sat at the table eating copious amounts of food. Lastly, a weedy-looking boy who wouldn't be out of place in a police lineup reclined on the table, his attention shifting like he was awaiting some sort of meeting and not simply skipping class.

"Well, look what we have here," said Weedy Boy. "Fresh meat—I mean freshmen." He laughed at his own joke, though no one else did.

Monson tried to keep his mouth shut. He was unsuccessful. "Seriously?"

Monson's eyebrow was raised so far he was in danger of losing it.

The boy's eyes narrowed, then he grinned. Monson returned the stare but tried to keep his face impassive, silently berating himself for his forked tongue. Suddenly, it was as if the group of seniors seemed to multiply into a few dozen. Had they been hiding, just waiting for such an opportunity, or had they been there the whole time? Regardless, they did not look happy; curse his wretched tongue.

The crowd of older boys circled Monson and his two friends as Weedy Boy spoke. "Freshman, didn't you know that you're not allowed down this hall?"

"Oh, sorry," said Casey, cutting off Monson's reply. He sounded polite and contrite, as if he wanted only to rectify any misunderstanding. Actually, he sounded a little *too* contrite. "We didn't realize that this was *your* hallway."

"I don't like your tone. You should be a little more respectful when addressing your elders."

"Well, you *shouldn't* like my tone," said Casey in an equally polite voice. "It's called sarcasm; look it up. It's a good word to know."

"You have quite the mouth on you," Weedy Boy glared at Casey. "I think we may have to teach you some manners."

That simple comment was enough to cause a dramatic change in the atmosphere surrounding the encounter; this could get ugly very quickly.

Not good, thought Monson as he took a step back, trying to create some space between himself and the upperclassmen. They, however, were not going to let him off the hook that easily. As Monson took a step back, they merely took a step forward. Monson was not particularly scared of a fight, however. After the horrors of his dreams, the threats from a bunch of rich kids pretending to be thugs did not mean much to him. He and his friends were, however, outnumbered, and it probably was not the best idea to get into a fight on the first day of school. Furthermore, based on his experience the day before, Monson could see his two friends doing something crazy like pulling out sticks and thrashing people indiscriminately. Considering Casey's freakish strength, that could be bad. Trying to talk his way out of this was probably his best bet. They didn't have anything against him personally...right?

The tension was high, but distraction and relief arrived in the form of a second group of students.

There were a good number of them; many girls lined the hall, most of whom wore their uniforms artfully, revealing just a bit more than the school code probably allowed. Directly behind them, an assortment of thuggish boys—the kind who solved everything with a well-placed fist. Clusters of younger and smaller boys who looked like lackeys of some sort teetered around, walking close enough to the group that people noticed, but far enough away that their presence was easy to ignore until needed. The group revolved around a tall boy who was basking in the admiration of foreign-looking twin girls, one on each arm. His brown hair was untidy, but strategically so, as if he had spent a great deal of time on it. He was wearing slightly shaded sunglasses, not unlike the ones Casey had taken from Kylie just that morning. His shirt was unbuttoned to right above mid-chest. While Monson assumed he was trying to look cool, he wasn't quite sure that the boy pulled it off.

"Mauller," the new boy barked at Weedy Kid. "Explain."

"Blow it out your tailpipe, Derek," Mauller's eyes narrowed. "This doesn't concern you."

"You're in *my* hallway," said Derek pompously. "Or did you forget who you were talking to?"

"Excuse me," broke in Monson. "I hate to interrupt this riveting show of comparative masculinity, but seeing as we have nothing to do with this, we would really like to be on our way."

"And who are you?" The new boy turned his attention to Monson with barely concealed disdain.

Monson gave Derek a polite smile. "It's rude to ask someone for his name without offering your own."

The boy looked like he was going to laugh for a moment—as if Monson had done something raucously inappropriate. All he managed was a smile, which did not reach his eyes; they remained cold and calculating.

"You must be new, and judging by your appearance, a 'shipper' to boot," Derek stated conclusively. "I wish they'd teach you scholarship children a thing or two before they allowed you in. Being the upstanding individual that I am, I'll educate you on the Roman custom for greetings. When someone of greater status honors you by speaking first in greeting or interrogation, it is customary to answer with your name and occupation, thus showing the proper respect to your superior."

"Really," said Monson. "So you're suggesting that you have greater status than I."

Monson spoke not to the boy but to Casey. "Did you get the memo on that? Because I don't remember voting."

Casey shrugged. "It was probably rigged anyway."

Monson knew he was being vicious. He simply did not care at this point.

"Apparently you don't know who I am, because if you did, we wouldn't be having this conversation. But even if you're uneducated in social pleasantries, I'd have thought who I am was obvious." Derek's rapturous smile returned to his face, and he squeezed the two foreign blondes on his arms. The girls squealed. "I'd get caught up on the customs of your school, freshman. You know what they say: 'When in Rome....'"

"Hmmm," Monson looked thoughtfully at Derek. "You know that's funny. I've never heard of that custom. What period is it from?"

Derek's smile faded a bit and his eyes narrowed, but he didn't say anything.

"Oh, don't tell me, you aren't just spouting something you heard? Please don't say you don't even know where the custom came from or why they had it?"

"It was from the early part of the Roman Republic," retorted Derek spitefully. "I would have—"

"A.D. or B.C.?" interrupted Monson.

"A.D." Derek's smirk was becoming outrageous.

"Now you're just guessing," said Monson, laughing. "If you don't know, why not just say so?"

"Why you little—"

"For your information, the Roman Republic only existed until the mid-part of the second century B.C., when Julius Caesar overthrew it. From that point on, it was an empire, which existed in the West in Rome until the fifth century, and in the East in Constantinople until the fourteenth century. Oh, and there never was a customary practice of greeting in the Roman caste system. Most of the time, the Senators and other important people didn't even acknowledge the commoners, let alone actually speak to them. What you're spouting is probably some jumped-up school tradition created to make the upperclassmen happy or to help other *special* individuals like yourself feel important. And while we're on the subject, we are not *in* Rome, so I hope you'll forgive me for not doing what the Romans do. Seeing as you don't really know anyway."

A thick silence settled on the crowd of students. Derek looked as if he had been smacked, while Mauller and his group of friends gazed on in shock. Monson wondered if he had gone too far and would now have to fight his way out. He considered the prospect of having the crap beat out of him on the first day of school as he looked at the arrogant jerk in front of him. Totally worth it. Might as well finish it properly

"My name is Monson Grey. Nice to meet you," Monson gave a little bow. "Now, if you will excuse me? I think my friends and I are probably already late."

Monson started to move past Derek, but Derek slammed a hand in front of him, blocking his path.

"Grey, you say? As in the—"

"New *Horum Vir*," said Monson, finishing Derek's sentence. "That's right."

Derek sneered as he eyed Monson. "These past months haven't been good to you. I remember you being prettier."

Monson felt a flush of anger. "Sorry to disappoint, but you shouldn't worry, Derek, was it? Right now, you're the prettiest girl at the ball."

Derek's sneer took a turn for the deadly. "I think you and I should have another chat somewhere a bit more private."

And there it was. It was time to throw down.

"What do you think you're doing?" inquired a vaguely familiar voice.

Everyone, including Derek, who flushed bright red, apparently recognizing the voice, turned to the newcomer. A group of familiar upperclassman girls pushed their way through. They looked scandalized—like the very thought of such bullying was unspeakable. Monson, thankful for the distraction, was about to make his exit when someone spoke to him.

"Don't tell me you aren't happy to see me?"

A soft hand caught his. The touch was so inviting, he instinctively turned. He saw a field of strawberry blonde hair and emerald green eyes watching him earnestly.

Taris Green.

"So, we meet again," she said with a gentle smile. "You seem to have a knack for being at the wrong place at the wrong time."

"You aren't telling me anything I don't know." Monson returned her smile. "I was just about to make my escape. Care to join me?"

She laughed, and it sounded more genuine than her laughter the previous day. She wiped at a corner of her eye. "I think this time *you* are hitting on *me*, Mr. Grey."

"Yes, how improper of me." Monson bowed. "I hope you won't hold it against me."

"I'm sorry to interrupt," said Derek sarcastically. "But do you know each other?"

"Of course," said Taris, keeping her eyes firmly on Monson, a fact that was not wasted on Derek. "Mr. Grey and I go way back."

"Oh yeah," agreed Monson, trying not to laugh. "*Way* back."

Derek continued to eye them suspiciously. Before he could say anything else, Taris opened her bag.

"I have something for you." She took a small box out of her bag and handed it to Monson. "It's part of your award. I don't know if you have one already, but the school provides this one so they can always get ahold of you."

Monson opened the box, a bit embarrassed by everyone watching.

"A cell phone? Why would I need one of those?"

"I'm just the Student Senate's messenger," said Taris with a shrug. "I just do what I'm told."

"You just do as you're told? I find that hard to believe."

She stuck her tongue out at him in a playful way.

Monson absentmindedly pulled out the phone and turned it on. It was very nice as far as cell phones go—thin, black, and slick. The phone even greeted him by name when he turned it on. "Hey, I already have someone's number in here," said Monson, slightly confused. "I thought this was a new phone. Why would it have a number in it?"

"Oh, you don't have to worry about that," said Taris, as she took a step closer to him. Behind her, Monson watched Derek's fists ball up in anger. "I put my number in your phone. You know, in case you have any questions."

The reaction to this was oddly profound. The twin boys against the wall started whispering to each other with hurried voices in a language no one else understood. Mauller whistled and glared spitefully at Derek. Derek's face flushed with anger. The rest of the girls just gaped at Taris, dumbfounded.

Monson surveyed the group's reactions. He suddenly had the impression that everyone in the room wanted to hurt him. It was not a pleasant experience.

"Thanks for this," said Monson, raising the phone. He then clicked a button and listened as Taris' phone rang. She grabbed it and held it up so only Monson could see the name. "My Hero," it read. He looked at her inquiringly, to which she just gave an enigmatic smile and a wink.

He caught the name she was under in his phone. "My *Princess*?"

Taris' smile took a turn for the wicked. "Only very special people get to call me that. That number is up to two now. Consider yourself lucky. I'm out like a daddy light. Bye-bye, Mr. Grey."

Taris turned and walked away without another word, but not without looking back. Derek's expression was murderous. Monson decided they should leave, and he, Artorius, and Casey walked in silence until they were sure they were out of earshot. Only then did the conversation finally start up again.

"I think we just found the main antagonist," said Casey, looking behind him. "Thinks a lot of himself, that one."

"And perhaps an initial love interest, too?" Artorius rubbed at his chin. "Grey, you lucky bastard."

"What in the world are you two talking about?" exclaimed Monson, totally confused. "You act as if we're in a movie or something."

They both laughed at this, though Monson couldn't see what was so funny.

"Right on, Grey!" said Artorius, looking over at Casey. "Gooney Boy over there wants to be a filmmaker, novelist, and *mangaka*. He always talks like that. You'd better be careful; he's probably already working on a screenplay of your life story."

"I couldn't do that," said Casey with mock disappointment. He wore the same look of exaggerated contrition that he used when they were talking to Derek. Monson waited patiently for the punchline. When none came, he asked,

"OK, I'll play along. Why can't you write this story?"

"Isn't that obvious?"

"Not really."

Casey's expression changed to a mix of pity and understanding.

"I can't write this story because I'm the main character. That would just be tacky."

"Wait...what?" asked Monson, running his hand through his hair. "How can you be the main character in the story of my life? Wouldn't I be the main character?"

"Well, traditionally, yes," said Casey in a very matter-of-fact voice. "But I demoted you because you're so boring."

That comment got Casey a smack on the arm and helped to dispel some of the lingering tension.

"So if I'm not the main character," asked Monson. "What am I?"

"Comic relief," said Casey, narrowing his eyes in a very comical way. "Don't worry. I'll give you some good one-liners."

CHAPTER 10
THE VOICE

UPON ARRIVING in their first class, the trio took seats at the back of the room. Casey and Artorius followed an already irritated Monson, who simply wanted to avoid bringing attention to himself. Because it was the first day, many of the students arrived early, waiting for the teacher to show up and start class. They talked in low voices, unpacking computers and tablets while they waited—in vain, as it turned out, as the start of class came and went with no teacher.

"Where the heck is she?" whispered Monson, although he didn't know why, as there wasn't anyone in the classroom who cared if he talked.

"I don't know," Casey whispered back. "I heard that she's a little weird. Maybe she's planning a sort of dramatic entry. You know, music, lights, and such."

"Oh, you'd love that, wouldn't you?" Monson placed a binder on his desk. "You and your movie mania."

"Of course," replied Casey indignantly. "I maintain that life would be a great deal more interesting if people broke out in random song and dance, supported by a laugh track."

"You're mental. You know that, right?"

"Ask me no questions, I'll tell you no lies."

"That doesn't make any sense."

They lapsed into silence, though the room was far from quiet, the students getting more boisterous as class time continued to tick away.

"Where could she be?" asked a pale, frumpy-looking boy in the front row.

"Maybe she's sick?"

"Isn't there a fifteen-minute rule?"

"This is BS!"

"Well, she'd better get here soon," said Monson, "or she's going to have a mass walkout. Probably not the best thing to happen on the first day of class."

"I'm sure she's coming," said Artorius absentmindedly, flipping through his textbook. "My cousin told me Ms. Blake has a great love for theatrics. Apparently, last year she showed up in a gorilla suit."

"Creepy," said Casey. "She must have been a drama major in college. Only people that can't cut it in the outside world pull crap like that. I mean really—" A snicker from his other side cut him off and made them all shift in their chairs.

A girl with lank, shoulder-length brown hair and thick, square glasses with ridiculously large rims sat next to them, giggling as she looked down at the same textbook as Artorius. Her eyes were a bit on the glassy side.

"Whoa," said Casey in surprise. "Where'd you come from?"

The girl blasted him with a face full of pout. "I've been here since you sat down. Am I really that unworthy of notice?"

Her voice sounded overwhelmingly forlorn.

Casey cocked his head to the left, clearly indicating that was exactly what he thought. Monson punched him on the arm.

"Ouch! What was that for, Grey?"

"You know dang well what that was for."

Casey held up his hands. "OK, OK, I wasn't going to say anything."

Monson turned towards the girl, searching for something to say. He saw the book she was reading.

"So, do you like to read?"

The girl did not answer at once. She continued to look at her book, and then turned towards Monson. To everyone's surprise, she asked, "Aren't you the new *Horum Vir*?" Her voice had changed, however; it now sounded girlish and annoyingly high-pitched. She also stared at his face with a mix of horror and wonder. This annoyed Monson. It annoyed him a great deal.

"Yeah," said Monson in surprise. He considered the girl for a moment, studying her slightly protuberant eyes. "You're familiar to me; have we met before?"

"I don't think so," said the girl with a coy little smile. "But I wouldn't mind getting to know you." She pushed her glasses further up the rim of her nose and gave him a slight wink.

Monson turned to Casey and Artorius, searching for some kind of guidance. They said nothing and just stared. When no help came, Monson returned his attention to the girl. "I'm flattered, but I don't even know your name. Why don't we start there?"

"Miranda," said the girl with an approving smile.

"Monson," he placed a hand on his chest. "This is Casey." He slapped Casey on the back. "And the oaf on the end is Arthur."

"Don't call me Arthur!" snapped Artorius.

"Pleased to meet you all." She stared at each of them in turn, giving them the chills. It was like she was sizing them up for some sort of show. Something about this girl didn't feel normal. She continued to scrutinize them before eventually settling on Monson.

"So how do you like Coren so far?"

"I can't complain." And really, he couldn't. "I have really nice living quarters. A really cool..." What was the word he used? "Manservant. And it seems like our teachers are going to be pretty cool."

"Oh really?" Miranda looked doubtful.

"Well, I guess. I can't really say for sure," conceded Monson. "I've only met one."

"And it doesn't seem that we're going to be meeting anymore, not this hour at least," interrupted Casey. "What a fruitcake. I could be working on my screenplay right now." He said this to no one in particular.

"Come on now, Casey," said Monson. "Let's not jump the gun. There could be any number of explanations for her being late."

"Yeah, like she's a nutbar dipped in crazy coating."

"You're hopeless."

"That's right, Casey," declared Miranda. "You really shouldn't judge without all the facts. Often your first impression isn't the correct one." She paused and looked off in the distance. Her eyes whipped back to Casey, "Then again, sometimes it is."

"What do you mean?" asked Casey, looking at the girl with an increasingly cynical eye. "What kind of a teacher lets their students sit alone for twenty minutes on the first day of classes?"

The girl gave him a sly little grin but did not answer. It was in that moment that Monson had to wonder if...no, it couldn't be.

"I don't know," Miranda said, turning her attention back to her book, "One trying to prove a point."

"What could that point," he gestured to the waiting students, "possibly be?"

"I think you should probably figure that out for yourself. Cassius."

Wait a minute, thought Monson. Cassius.

Casey made to answer but was interrupted by Monson. "I don't think you want to say anything else, *Cassius*."

"Why are you calling me—"

"Very good, Mr. Grey." Miranda's tone was again different. It sounded cool and rich, but with traces of the young girlish undertone from moments ago. "You have been very helpful in proving my point. I was told you were a sharp one. When did you figure it out?"

Monson looked at her keenly. "I think I knew from the beginning."

He hadn't really, but he thought he might as well own it. One good thing was, he did know where he recognized her from: orientation.

Artorius and Casey gaped in absolute bewilderment. Monson just laughed.

"Oh, boys. You are indeed missing something. But I'm sure it will be made clear momentarily." Miranda pulled off her glasses, which she apparently did not need. She peered at them with deep smoldering eyes that were at odds with her lank hair. How had he not noticed such eyes?

"So, now what happens?" asked Monson.

"I'll show you." The girl stood up. She remained next to her seat as she righted herself, smoothing out her top and straightening her skirt. She walked towards the front of the classroom. Other people in the classroom started to notice. The idle chatter died down as people watched, curious as to what this girl would do.

Miranda stood in front of the class, a calm, grounded expression on her face. It was vastly different from her previous flighty demeanor. Evidently, her acting was better than Casey originally thought. She smiled at the different students who seemed to finally comprehend what was happening. She turned and wrote on the blackboard.

"My name is Miranda Blake." She wrote her name on the blackboard at the same time she spoke. "You may call me Miranda. Any questions so far?"

No one in the room spoke.

"Excellent," Miranda said, dipping back into her flighty voice. "I have a question that I want you to all ponder before we call roll and review the syllabus."

Monson chanced a glance at the rest of his classmates, who looked mildly interested. He noticed Artorius' eyes suddenly grow very large. Slowly, Monson turned back to their professor.

Professor Blake had removed her hair—which just happened to be a wig. Long, blonde curly hair, not unlike Kylie's, was bound in a net-like piece of cloth. She let the confined curls fall, and with this simple action, Miranda Blake captured the attention of her class.

———

THE REST of that first day—the classes, people, and interactions— were disjointed and distinctly new. Given his memory loss, this fact was probably a safe assumption. However, there was nothing familiar about this traditional school setting. It was definitely something new for him, even if he couldn't remember for sure.

His lack of memories notwithstanding, Monson felt his next two classes were relatively...well, normal, at least compared with his first class. His Applied Mathematics class, taught by a sickly-looking but very nice woman named Sally Masters, felt like a necessary evil. The class was hard, very hard in fact. Sally herself looked like she was falling apart at the seams. Monson was almost positive that she was at least partially blind. Despite her appearance, however, Professor Masters was vigorous. Vigorous to the point where she made students do push-ups if they answered a question incorrectly. (Monson ended up doing a lot of push-ups that day.) She also gave them a boatload of homework.

Next was Science, which took the freshman students to the far side of the campus. A massive building that doubled as the county's hospital housed one of the most advanced health care facilities in the nation. In this facility, students received the rare privilege of learning from a range of leading experts in both the social and physical sciences. Monson learned that for their first few weeks, Professor Scott Lucas, a bioengineer from the University of Washington, would handle their Biology class, while Dr. Henry Cast, a Ph.D. and professor at Bowling Green University, would lecture them on sociology. The two professors were very knowledgeable without a hint of personality. It was all very impressive. Yet, it was so—

"Boring!" yelled Casey, as they walked out of the building an hour and a half later. Monson scanned their surroundings, hoping they were far enough away that they would not be overheard.

"Ugh," continued Casey. "If we have to sit through another one of those lectures, I might have to take myself to the top of Mt. Rainier and jump off!"

"Well, that's just silly," said Monson amusedly.

"Don't try and stop me, Grey," said Casey dramatically. "I have no intention—"

"Casey."

"Of allowing their artistic repression—"

"Casey!"

"To dampen my poetic spirit—"

"CASEY!"

Casey abruptly stopped talking. "What?"

"I don't plan on stopping you."

"What?"

"I said, I don't plan on stopping you."

Casey looked baffled at this.

"What do you mean, you don't plan on stopping me?"

Monson sighed. "If you want to throw yourself from the top of Mt. Rainier, I don't plan on stopping you. I was just going to say that any of the buildings here would suffice for a venture of that type. You only need a couple of stories to fall from, especially if you go headfirst. Going all the way to Mt. Rainier would be a waste of gas; you should be more worried about global warming."

They looked at each other, then without warning started to laugh. Others joined in, which surprised Monson. It seemed that already Casey was very popular. Actually, people who probably did not even hear their exchange started to laugh, including a girl with short, sassy brown hair and light brown eyes. She smiled at them as she passed and made eye contact with Monson. Her smile was a bit on the wicked side.

"Who is that?" Artorius turned to Monson. "Grey, do you know her?"

"Can't say that I do."

"She's really pretty."

Monson started to reply but stopped when he noticed a strange glint in Artorius' eye.

Artorius advanced very quickly, leaving Monson and Casey in the midst of Casey's adoring crowd. Monson leaned toward Casey.

"What on earth was that about?"

Casey looked a little uncomfortable. He sighed.

"Artorius...he wants a girlfriend."

Monson waited, thinking that surely that could not be all there was to it, but Casey did not say anything else.

"He wants a girlfriend?"

"Yeah," answered Casey. "He wants a girlfriend."

"Umm...I feel like I missed something there."

"It's a long story."

"I'll take your word for it."

"That would be best."

The two of them did not see Artorius again until well into lunch. Monson and Casey found a spot in the back corner of the cafeteria where they tried to remain unnoticed by their fellow classmates. Monson felt this said something about Casey. He was not the type of person to bask in the admiration of others. For the most part, people sat apart from them, with the exception of the boy in the wheelchair that Monson attempted to help earlier that day. Wheelchair boy ignored them, and they him, even though they were sitting next to one another. About forty minutes after they sat down, Artorius finally showed up.

"Where were you?" exclaimed Monson and Casey in unison, the latter actually spitting out food.

Artorius did not say anything. He just sat and arranged his food, but instead of eating, he just stared at his plate, looking happy.

Monson spoke to him. "Artorius …are you OK?"

Artorius turned to look at him. "OK? I'm freaking great!"

"You didn't answer our question," said Casey. "Where were you this whole time?"

Artorius gave him a devilish grin. "It's a surprise; you'll see."

Monson hated when people said things like that.

They finished their food, Artorius eating with gusto, as he did not have much time. Twenty minutes later, the boys found themselves at The GM's main entrance. Casey stopped there and gestured.

"We're down this way." He pointed towards the direction of The Barracks. "You gonna be all right on your own? You sure you don't want us to walk with you?"

Monson's eyes narrowed, but he smiled. "Of course not. I wouldn't want you to ruin my rep."

Both Artorius and Casey laughed. "All right, we'll meet up with you later. Don't get lost."

They left, Casey still attempting to force out of Artorius where he went.

Monson watched them leave, feeling slightly apprehensive. Going to Mr. Gatt's history class by himself had seemed like a good idea when he signed up, but now they were actually leaving—no, he should not think that way. He would be fine.

It took some time to find, but eventually Monson neared a small brick building surrounded by a grove of trees and a hedge. Detached from the main portion of Coren's campus, the classroom seemed out of place on Coren's campus, but nice at the same time. The scenery was very peaceful, and the combination of pine, weeping willow, and a variety of flowers created an unusually lovely and fresh aroma. It lightened Monson's heart a great deal, making him forget his worries ever so briefly.

His mind drifted for a time until a voice rang out from under a patch of trees, interrupting his solitude. Tentatively, he spoke.

"Hello?"

No answer came. He echoed his greeting.

"Hello?" Again, no answer.

He moved closer to where he thought the sound came from when he heard it again. A beautiful voice rang out, clear, clean, and harmonious, as if it was creating its own accompanying notes. Monson wandered, searching, as the music rose and fell. He stopped and peered through the drapes of a willow tree and saw a girl with long dark hair standing maybe fifty feet in the distance. Monson wished he could make out the words as he found the melody very appealing; though he was standing close enough to hear her voice, he was too far away to hear the actual verse. Monson continued to listen and allowed his mind to wander. Suddenly, the girl turned.

Oh crap! thought Monson as he ducked behind a tree. Luckily, the girl turned away from him. She must not have noticed him standing there. Something odd crept over him. A feeling, the murmur of a heart pulsating within him. It brought up images of faces and places he did not recognize. He closed his eyes, and the last thing he saw was a tree-covered mountain that seemed to call to him from a distance.

The girl stopped singing, and the sight vanished. Monson opened his eyes and chanced a look, hoping to see the girl's face. He wanted to know who she was.

"What are you doing?"

Turning quickly, Monson slipped and fell hard on his rear end. It hurt. Embarrassed, he twisted to see the boy in the wheelchair staring at him with mild interest on his face. Monson recognized him immediately and cringed, thinking about their earlier encounter. The boy had dirty blond hair, light blue eyes, and soft features, which gave him a somewhat feminine appearance. Monson made a mental note not to say that. Beyond this, his eyes projected strength, and Monson comprehended a single dominant feature emanating from the boy's countenance: *Intelligence. Overwhelming intelligence.*

As he looked into the boy's eyes, Monson's vision blurred, which forced him to blink. The boy's eyes did not so much as flicker, but

Monson sensed a certain degree of remorse. Remembering the girl, Monson spun on his feet, hoping to get a glance. She was gone. Monson turned back towards the boy and finally answered the question.

"Yeah…that wasn't what it looked like."

The boy smiled at this. "So you weren't spying?"

Monson thought about it for a moment, then sighed. "OK, maybe it was exactly what it looked like."

"At least you picked a cute one." The boy looked close to laughing.

Monson shrugged. "I wouldn't know. I didn't see her face."

"Too bad for you. Shall we go?"

The boy turned abruptly, moving his chair with amazing speed. Startled by the sudden end of the conversation, it took Monson a moment to recover, by which time the boy was already quite far in front of him. Monson scrambled after him, ignoring his clothes, thoroughly disheveled from falling down. They moved quickly up the path toward the front door of the building. As they neared the entrance, Monson hesitated, not knowing if the boy would accept his help this time. Monson decided it did not matter and rushed forward, catching the door handle and swinging it open right as the wheelchair rolled through it.

"Nice one, Grey." The boy continued rolling down the hall.

"Thanks," Monson muttered, stepping through the door himself. He rushed after the boy and caught up to him halfway down the hall.

"You're really fast on that thing," Monson stammered this through puffs of air as he struggled to keep up with the wheelchair.

"Have to be," answered the boy. "They don't give us very long between classes, do they?"

"That's certainly true. I think I've been late to almost every class."

"Well, spying on girls doesn't help."

"Shut up."

They entered the classroom.

CHAPTER 11
A TEACHER LIKE NONE OTHER

THE BELL RANG as the two entered a very large room. It did not look like a traditional classroom but was long and rectangular, almost like a lodge of some sort. The deeply stained polished wood floor gave the room an ancient feel. The same brick Monson saw on the outside of the building was inside as well, giving a clear indication of the building's age. Windows draped with ivy outside lined the wall and bathed the students in an earthy ambiance. It was nice, but he wondered why the building was here at all. Everything else on campus was new. Why keep this?

As a boy bumped into him on his way into the classroom, Monson suddenly remembered he was late. He scanned the room full of older students still milling around, chatting idly. A large group congregated near the front of the room around someone he could not see. He spotted an empty seat in the back corner and started for it, glancing over his shoulder at the boy in the wheelchair. The boy smiled and nodded, indicating that Monson should continue. Monson made a beeline for the seat.

How uncomfortable. He could actually feel the eyes of the older students sitting around him, many gazing at him in distaste. The boy in the wheelchair was looking at him from across the room. Monson smiled, and the boy nodded back, then shifted his chair forward.

Crap, thought Monson, letting his attention trail off. He had forgotten to ask the boy his name, though he should not be too hard on himself; their conversation was not exactly extensive. Monson felt pleased by the boy's change in attitude from when he tried to help him earlier. Monson stopped as something occurred to him. The boy had said "Grey" in the hall. That could not be right. Monson did not remember telling him his name. How did he know? He racked his brain trying to remember if he had seen him at the assembly or the reception. Consequently, he found the chattering of the students very annoying.

A creak sounded as Mr. Gatt entered the room carrying a large box. The sound caught Monson's attention, and he looked up towards the door. Mr. Gatt looked as slick as ever in the same dark blue three-piece suit. He placed the box on the table and opened it, still not speaking, not even looking at the class. Most of the chattering died down as the students became interested in what Mr. Gatt was doing. After the box was open, he reached inside and fiddled around with some unknown objects. He pulled out two glossy sheets that looked like posters and set them facedown on the table. Monson tried to get a look at them, but Mr. Gatt moved too quickly. Monson had an inkling that he did not want the class to see. The teacher smiled a toothy grin as he surveyed the class.

"Good afternoon, everyone. Welcome to my class." He looked excited, almost buoyant. "We should start with the roll. I don't know all your names; the class is bigger than I expected."

There were far more people than Monson had anticipated as well. He looked around counting, although his back corner seat made it difficult to see everyone. As far as he could tell, there were at least thirty students, probably more. That was odd. What normal, healthy high school student wants to take a class in analytical history? Monson finally looked to the seat beside him. He gawked.

"Were you always there?" A pair of deep green eyes sparkled as they peered into his. "No, I saw you sit down and thought I would come and keep you company."

Monson's eyes narrowed a bit. "Now why would you do that?"

She smiled her wicked smile. "Why do *you* think I would do that?"

Monson had no idea. This girl could not be interested in *him*, could she? No, of course not. He blurted out without thinking, "I don't know, my *dashing* good looks?"

She laughed but did not answer. She simply adjusted herself in the chair, a very innocent look on her face. She then gave her wholehearted attention to Mr. Gatt, which annoyed Monson a great deal; he hated being ignored.

Monson spied on the girl sitting next to him: Taris Green. Green eyes, long strawberry-blond hair, and soft, creamy skin. She was smoldering, like just being near her could overpower you. Her looks, her flowery perfume, her temperament; it was all very appealing. And everyone thought so. This was the current "It" girl. The daughter of some famous Hollywood actor, Taris' popularity as *the* teen idol was quickly gaining momentum as she appeared in movies and on television and gained recognition as a singer. Many of the guys on the campus had never even seen her in person, despite living in the same city and attending the same school. Taris Green was one of the truly elite and until now opted to take private lessons from tutors. Her reasons? Unknown. But regardless, the girl was known to be kind and gentle, the perfect balance of supermodel and Mother Teresa.

This information was all new to Monson, of course. He happened to overhear a conversation about her in the hallways and even saw a rather risqué poster of her pulled up on someone's laptop. Monson blushed crimson at the thought of it and then immediately scolded himself for blushing. He sighed. Monson was well aware of his appearance and less-than-desirable social status. So why would this girl go out of her way to talk to him? He just did not understand it.

Monson forced himself to abandon his surveillance activities when the tap of chalk hitting a chalkboard became too distracting. Mr. Gatt was beginning his lecture. Wait; Mr. Gatt said he was going to take roll. Did Monson miss it? Monson hoped fervently that Mr. Gatt didn't count him absent. He looked to the board and saw three words written in a neat scroll:

Fact. Truth. Belief.

"I want all of you to take out a piece of paper," Mr. Gatt said, turning towards them.

They did so with a great deal of shuffling.

"Is everyone ready? Good." He looked at the class and, grabbing one of his posters, turned his back to them again, saying, "Write the definition of these three words." He pointed at each.

Fact, truth, belief. Huh? thought Monson, studying his own paper where the three words were written. *What do those words mean?* If he was being honest with himself, he had never really thought about what those words meant. He just knew. Monson looked at Mr. Gatt. A poster was now hanging from the top of the chalkboard. It looked like a reproduction of an oil painting. An old one, probably 17th century, though Monson couldn't say for sure. He had recently watched a History Channel special about painters through the ages, and this painting reminded him of some of the works on that program from that period. Monson looked closer, leaning as far forward in his chair as he could. The picture depicted an older man standing pleasantly in his frame. He was wearing a funny pointed hat that was midnight blue and accented with golden trim. A long white beard with streaks of silver hung to mid-chest and contrasted nicely with a star-covered robe of the same color as the hat. The man leaned against a wall with a very serene look on his face. Monson heard Taris breathe out of the corner of her mouth.

"He looks like a wizard." She looked amused.

Monson did not say anything but scrutinized the picture more closely. It did look like a wizard; however, Monson was saved the trouble of guessing further when Mr. Gatt spoke.

"Mr. Peter Shaarin." Mr. Gatt spoke softly, but it sounded like a command. "Will you tell me, perchance, what you wrote down for the word *fact?*"

Monson heard a boy with a heavy accent speak but was unable to make out the words. Monson was not the only one. Other people in the class must have missed it as well, as many looked confused. Monson strained his ears, listening to the boy named Peter speak again, louder this time.

"A fact is something that actually exists. Something observable, you could say." He spoke with a thickly accented voice. Wanting to place a name with a face, Monson actually stood up slightly hoping to see Peter, but to no avail, as the boy's back was to him. This problem solved itself when Mr. Gatt next spoke to Peter.

"Excellent! That is as good as any definition I have heard. Will you come and write your answer on the board?"

As Mr. Gatt held out a piece of chalk, Peter reluctantly stood and walked forward, taking the chalk. He wrote his definition in neat curlicue handwriting under the word *fact*. He handed the chalk back and returned to his seat. Monson recognized him instantly. He was one of the boys who had held him up in the halls earlier that day. Monson felt a lurch in the pit of his stomach. This could be bad if some of those other boys were in here as well.

"Derek," Mr. Gatt gestured towards the middle of the front row of students. "What about you? What is your definition of truth?"

A smoothly arrogant voice shot out from the rows of students. Monson grimaced; he knew that voice. Derek was already answering.

"I think truth is a relative concept; there is no absolute truth or fact. But if I had to come to a real definition, then I would say truth means *conformity* with fact or reality. To follow truth is to follow fact or reality."

Monson gaped at the answer. It was deep and insightful. Derek had come across as such an idiot back in the hallway. It was quite obvious that he was not. Mr. Gatt also looked pleased with the answer.

"Interesting answer, Mr. Dayton. Will you write that on the board?"

Like Peter, Derek moved to the board and wrote out his answer. He turned back toward the students and started to walk to his seat, his eyes scanning the room. He stopped suddenly, almost comically, as he gazed upon Monson. His gaze flickered, and an angry flush washed over his face. Monson's gaze dropped, and he focused on Mr. Gatt's voice.

"How about you, Miss Green? Please round out our definitions."

The mention of Taris' name had a noticeable effect on the room, as the students tensed. Taris either did not notice or did not care, as she appeared unruffled, her expression playful, a sassy smile continuing to the edges of her full lips. She stood up and moved to the front of the classroom, well aware that every boy in the room was staring at her with hearts in their eyes, while the girls did their best to maintain their self-confidence in the midst of royalty. She took the chalk from Mr. Gatt, smiling and giving him a full blast of her charm. He smiled but rolled his eyes slightly. She wrote one word on the board.

Conviction.

Taris handed the chalk back to Mr. Gatt and slowly walked back to her seat. The room remained incredibly quiet.

"Well done, Miss Green," said Mr. Gatt, looking from her answer to the girl. "I could not have said it better myself."

She nodded her head towards him as if to accept the compliment. Mr. Gatt continued.

"These are the ideas that we will be studying this year; the differences between fact and truth and the respective effect of belief on both. Why do we recognize some things as fact yet other things as truth? Are they the same? Are they different? What does belief have to do with fact or truth? How do the three affect each other? This class will look at facts, beliefs, and truths in the hopes of coming to a better under-standing of each. Any questions?"

No one raised a hand. Monson understood why. Mr. Gatt's voice had suddenly become quite appealing, like his words were going through special ears on your body. When one listened with these ears, what was said could not be ignored; one could only listen and understand.

"If there are no questions, then we will move on to this." Mr. Gatt pointed towards the picture behind him. "Who can tell me who this is?"

Several hands shot in the air, including Taris'. Mr. Gatt looked surprised but then laughed.

"OK, let me rephrase the question. Who can tell me who this is without referring to a certain popular children's book we all know and love?"

Everyone, including Taris, put their hands down. Monson raised an eyebrow at this. She crinkled her nose and stuck out her tongue at him. He laughed.

Monson raised his hand. The portrait suddenly reminded him of something he saw while in the hospital. Mr. Gatt called on him, looking pleased.

"Yes, Mr. Grey, do you have an answer for us?"

Monson hesitated, then said softly, "The Sword in the Stone."

This statement was met with a shocked silence. Mr. Gatt, however, seemed to understand. He gestured towards him as if to say, go on.

Monson hesitated again, understanding how odd this probably sounded.

"There was a movie made many years ago about a boy who had to pull a sword out of a stone to become the new King of England. The boy had a wizard helping him. His job was to guide the boy in becoming one of the greatest rulers of all time. The wizard's name was Merlin."

Comprehension was starting to dawn on the listeners, which

caused whispers to erupt all over the classroom, drowning out the last of Monson's words.

"Well done, Mr. Grey, well done."

Students continued to whisper among themselves. Mr. Gatt held up a hand for silence and again spoke to Monson.

"You must have watched a lot of T.V. when you were *resting*."

People were staring at him, literally turning in their seats so they could look at him. He dropped his eyes.

"You could say that." Monson hoped that Mr. Gatt would drop it.

The teacher seemed to sense Monson's hesitancy as he moved closer to the poster and pointed to the man in the picture.

"What if I told all of you that this is Merlin?"

People burst out laughing at this. The sense of foreboding as Mr. Gatt queried Monson vanished with this question. Even Monson laughed, knowing quite well that Merlin was a fictional character perpetuated by King Arthur legends.

"I am quite serious." Mr. Gatt's words cut them off. Even their thoughts seemed to skid to a halt. The silence started to build again. In a quiet voice, Mr. Gatt continued.

"Who was Merlin?" He was looking towards the painting, slightly glassy-eyed. "Was there a man who created a legend or a legend that created a man? You must ask these questions. What are the facts, what is the truth, and how does our belief affect our perception? There are facts, there is truth, there is belief. We just need to find what all of them are."

The statement hung in the air. Suddenly the bell rang, startling the students. It felt as if they just sat down, but sure enough, class was over. People roused themselves, gathering personal belongings and making their way out the door. Taris stood up and gathered her things very slowly, as if she was waiting for something. This changed, however, when Derek Dayton started in their direction, and her pace sped up considerably.

Taris lifted her bag and faced Monson, who had yet to move. The full weight of her gaze fell upon him as she tossed her hair and then turned, looking over her shoulder.

"Later, pretty boy."

Monson just stared after her, as mystified by her behavior as ever. Derek gave him a really nasty look and then gave chase. Finally, Monson grabbed his stuff and walked towards the front of the room. As he neared the door, Mr. Gatt spoke.

"So what did you think, Mr. Grey?" His voice was pleasant but curious, as if he really wanted to know Monson's opinion.

"Interesting," replied Monson. "I'm curious where you are going with all this."

Mr. Gatt smiled. "As you should be. Be prepared, Grey, this is gonna be one hell of a ride." Monson's jaw dropped at the expression.

With that, he left, leaving Monson staring after him and beginning to understand why so many people had signed up for this class. Mr. Gatt was like no one he had ever met.

CHAPTER 12
BOKKEN

"YO, HERO!" said Casey, greeting Monson the second he walked into the gym. Casey looked at him curiously. "Dude, what the flying flip took ya so long? Coach Able has already called roll."

"I couldn't find the dumb place! Who puts a huge brand-spanking-new stadium in the middle of the freaking forest? Seriously?" demanded Monson.

"Yeah, I know what you mean," said Casey, with a knowing look on his face. "But you have to admit that though the location sucks, a dedicated stadium is pretty sick."

"Yeah, you got me there," admitted Monson. "If this is the Training Ground, I can't imagine what the Battlefield looks like."

The "Training Ground" was more akin to a multi-sport complex than a typical high school gym, and Monson could have sworn that most of the school was here. Students were scattered all over the place, engaged in various activities. Some played volleyball or basketball. Several others were dressed in karate gi or fencing attire. It was quite the sight.

"The *Battleground*, Monson! It's called the Battleground, and it's where Coren plays its football games. Everything else is The Training

Ground. You're standing in one of the most advanced indoor stadiums in the world. More than five billion dollars, dude, I kid you not."

It didn't surprise Monson; the place felt like it was chiseled from pure gold. Monson looked around and noticed a lot of people staring at him.

"Come on, bro-has. We'd better get you a locker and inform one of the coaches that you're here."

As they started off, Monson looked around. "How was your fifth period?"

Casey glanced in either direction. "I didn't go."

Monson turned to him. "Why not?"

Casey put his finger to his mouth, which plainly indicated he didn't want to talk about it right now.

Monson cocked an eyebrow. OK, Magnum, P.I., I'll play along.

They walked in silence as they made their way across the gym, through a large pair of doors marked "Men."

"Where's Artorius?" asked Monson.

"Over yonder somewhere talking to some chickadees," said Casey. "We need to find that boy a woman. I think he may lose it soon."

"Whatever that means," Monson chuckled. Then, remembering Kylie, Monson asked, "Speaking of women, Casey, when are you going to tell me what happened between you and Kylie?"

"We'd better hurry before we get busted." Casey sounded stressed as he quickened his pace.

"Oh, come on!" exclaimed Monson, rushing after him. The fact had not been lost on him that Casey was doing his best to blow him off, which made him even more curious.

Monson attempted to catch up with Casey, whose smile was more like a grimace, as if he was in pain. They arrived at the double steel doors at the same time that a group of boys dressed in dark blue gym shorts and plain white t-shirts came stumbling out, pushing one another around.

The last boy saw Casey walking towards them and, apparently

without thinking, held the door open while standing to one side. Casey acknowledged this gesture with a simple nod of the head. He passed the boy, entering the locker room without a backward glance. A few steps behind Casey, Monson, too, was about to slide through the door.

He had just made it over the threshold when a sharp pain erupted in his head, neck, and upper back. A blow from the door hit him with enough force to make him stagger and drop to one knee. The ringing in his aching head echoed as he turned around to see what had happened: The boy stood in the doorway, leaning against the frame and laughing with his friends.

"You need to be more aware of your surroundings," said the boy as his friend patted him on the back. "If you aren't, bad things might happen. And we wouldn't want that, would we?"

His voice dripped with sarcasm.

"You're right." Monson glared at him, his voice very quiet. "We wouldn't want bad things to happen, as we might be held responsible for those bad things. And that would be even worse."

The boy looked shocked at Monson's words and his tone. Suddenly angry, he knelt down to Monson's level. He spoke equally softly.

"You'd better be careful, peasant. Your kind isn't wanted here. You should know your place and be aware of whom you are talking to before you get mouthy. Or didn't I hit you hard enough?"

Anger pulsed through Monson as he attempted to shake the pain from his head. His suspicions were confirmed; the strike from the door was on purpose. This should have thrown him into a state of confusion. Questions should have been erupting from within him as these unexplainable events unfolded.

This did not happen.

Far from clouding his thoughts, the boy's words helped Monson to channel his anger. His mind became clear and his focus sharp. Bloody images flashed past his eyes as his disgust and outrage infused him. He glared murderously. Even more frightening than his fear, confusion, or anger was the new feeling starting to emerge. It felt foreign and…dangerous. Monson tried to control it, but it filled him up, bringing him to the brink of rage. Slowly, painfully, something like a dam inside broke, and the sensation consumed him. Monson rose to his feet, tears of anger and repulsion flowing freely, as much from his internal struggle as his external injuries. He fought to keep the anger at bay.

The boys watched him. Monson witnessed arrogance give way to confusion, apprehension, then fear. Monson glared with the newfound fire within him. He walked towards the boys filled with purpose, yet without knowing what he was going to do nor caring about the consequences.

"MONSON!" A hand pulled at his shoulder, and Monson spun around to look Casey straight in the eye. "Snap out of it!"

Monson awoke; at least that's what it felt like. His energy slipped away from him, as if he had just run a marathon. He did not say anything but turned quickly back towards the boys in time to see the locker room doors slam shut. They were nowhere to be found. Monson slowly faced Casey, who just stood there gazing at him.

"What'd you do?" Casey looked at Monson apprehensively.

"Nothing," replied Monson defensively. "I asked them if they wanted to dance, but they said I wasn't good enough. Made me kind of angry."

"Grey!" Casey's voice sounded strained. "Now is not the time for joking. Why were you shaking? And why did those guys look like they were going to piss their pants?"

"Oh, don't exaggerate," said Monson dismissively. "I must have offended them somehow, so they thought they would give me some special treatment. I just wasn't in the mood."

Casey eyed Monson suspiciously; he was clearly skeptical of Monson's account.

Monson stopped and took a step closer to Casey. "Why are you getting on *my* case? I mean, I get whacked in the back of the head with a metal door, and you're acting like I just killed someone."

"Whacked in the head? What do you mean whacked in the head?"

Monson didn't answer.

"Sorry, dude." He sounded like he meant it. "Didn't mean to accuse you. It's just not very often that a group of five guys take off running right after they haze a younger student." He looked at Monson thoughtfully. "I don't know what happened, but something made them tuck tail and run."

"They probably saw a teacher or something," Monson shrugged. "Come on, we need to get out there before Artorius takes all the ladies."

"You mean before Artorius gets smacked."

They both laughed and returned to normal conversation, though Monson was preoccupied.

He had almost lost control to something so powerful and *dangerous*. Very dangerous—Monson thought back to the feeling and shook his head. That feeling, whatever it was, did not feel like *him*, but nonetheless was a part of him; it was something familiar, but at the same time foreign. Regardless of what it was, he hoped he didn't experience it again.

Casey stopped Monson in front of the giant steel door. "OK, so here is the thing about Coach Hawke before we go in."

Monson cocked an eyebrow. "What do you mean?"

Casey rubbed his face contemplatively. "Coach Hawke is...different. Just go with it."

Monson's eyebrow rose higher. "On that enigmatic note...."

Coach Hawke's office looked like a converted storage room. Large blackboards filled with potential plays and training schedules competed for space with piles of sports paraphernalia. Despite the room's contents, the boys felt like they were entering a club: Jazz music, played at high volume, reverberated in the enclosed space.

The man himself was sitting at a small desk, tapping lightly on his computer keyboard. He was a beast, large and rugged.

"Hey Coach Hawke," Casey yelled so he could be heard over the music. "I wanted to introduce you to the—"

Coach Hawke raised one massive finger to silence him. Eyes closed, the giant of a man sat in his chair, humming tunelessly to the jazz blaring from the music player.

Monson laughed while Casey gawked. Monson spoke quietly, "That's not something you see every day."

"Yeah, he's a bit of an eccentric," agreed Casey, not quite as softly.

"Should we come back later?"

"Maybe," Casey looked back towards the door. "Come on, you can just use my locker."

"At-ten-tion!"

They both jumped as the husky voice echoed threateningly around the small office. Coach Hawke, apparently finished with his meditation or whatever it was, now towered over them, his hard eyes leveled at Monson.

The boys quailed underneath the man's stare. They shot concerned looks at each other.

"This must be our new *Horum Vir*." Coach Hawke smiled. He sounded sincere, almost kind.

"Monson Grey," said Monson, stepping forward and offering his hand. "I am very happy to meet—" He was cut off when the huge man took him in his arms and squeezed him like a teddy bear.

"I am so happy to finally meet you." Monson thought the man was crying, although he could not be sure of this, as his own breathing suddenly became a far more pressing issue.

"This is a truly momentous occasion. A time when we can meet and greet one another like brothers and forge ahead in the style of my Germanic ancestors—"

"Co...ach Hawke," wheezed Monson through stabs of pain.

"We, like they once did, shall push forward, experience being our guide—"

"Coach...."

"I shall act as shepherd and you as sheep—"

"COACH!"

Coach Hawke stopped talking but maintained his iron hold on Monson.

"Did you say something, Grey?"

"I…can't…breathe."

"Oh, sorry, Grey," said Coach Hawke. He let go of Monson, who dropped to the ground hard, crumpling as he landed next to Casey. Coach Hawke grabbed Monson by his collar and hoisted him back up, suspending him a few inches above the ground before gently lowering him to the floor.

"Hey Coach," grinned Casey in amusement, "we need to get Monson a locker. Mind helping us out?"

"I would be overjoyed to help you out," replied Coach Hawke enthusiastically. "Follow me, boys."

Coach Hawke gave Monson a quick tour of the locker room, pointing out the showers, lockers, spa, and different therapy areas. Lastly, he showed Monson a strange sort of dispenser unit.

"And now," he began with a flourish, "may I present to you the clothing unit. This is where you pick up your gym clothes each day. You can put your dirty clothes in one of the bins over there." He pointed towards large blue bins on the opposite wall. "They'll be washed and returned to the dispenser. Any questions?"

Monson and Casey shook their heads.

"Then, until we meet again, I bid you farewell." He left whistling his jazz song from earlier.

Monson changed into the gym clothes, and then he and Casey emerged from the boys' locker room, Casey still chuckling about their encounter with Coach Hawke.

"He's an interesting one, isn't he?" said Monson as he strolled casually towards a large dark blue mat. Monson rubbed his rib cage almost instinctively. "I think he broke one of my ribs."

Casey renewed his laughter, trying to speak through gasps of air,

"Crazy, huh? Not what you'd expect from an ex-professional football player."

"Not at all. Wait—ex-professional football player?"

"Oh yeah, he used to play professionally until he got hurt. He was really good, too."

"Unexpected."

Casey nodded. "I know, right?"

"Hey, Casey, Monson!" Artorius came into view, closely followed by a small group of girls who all looked about their age.

"What took you guys so long?" inquired Artorius when he was finally close enough to them that he did not have to yell.

"Got lost," said Monson simply. Then, making a slight nod in their direction, "I see what you've been up to, Artorius. Who are your friends?"

"Indigo Harrison," replied a cute brunette with thick brown hair. Monson recognized her; she was the same girl Artorius had been so interested in earlier that day.

"Monson Grey." He smiled at her, his mind racing. "And who are your friends?"

Indigo turned and pointed while naming each girl.

"Christy Wayne," an asset-heavy blonde girl in a stretched-tight shirt who was not at all shy about her particular gifts.

"And Ignacio Anderson," a pale, skinny girl with very large, tawny-colored eyes.

Monson smiled and nodded at each girl. Their reactions to his appearance confused him. They looked disgusted, that much was sure, but also intrigued. Was he missing something?

Monson glanced at Artorius, who looked like a kid in a candy store —a really *big* candy store. He was eyeing Indigo expectantly, while she tried to avoid his gaze. An awkward silence settled after the introductions, not helped by Casey, who was trying desperately not to laugh.

Monson decided he had enough. "Well, ladies, it was nice meeting you all. I'm just going to go over here now."

He moved rather quickly to get away from the stares of Artorius' friends, whose eyes he could feel on his back.

At a comfortable distance, the crack of wood caught his attention. On a mat not far away, surrounded by students, two people were engaged in heated mock combat using large sticks crudely formed in the shape of swords. They resembled the ones that Casey and Artorius used the day before. Masked and covered in a weird kind of body armor, the two combatants strove against each other to gain dominance. The contest was short-lived: The shorter of the two fighters was far more skilled. His movements were small and sharp and almost totally defensive in nature; he took very few opportunities to counterattack. More often than not, he defended with a one-handed style, leaving the other hand draped to one side. This explained why he was using a shorter stick—a longer one would make this style of fighting difficult. The heavier opponent managed to land a few blows before an incredibly fast counter from the short combatant effectively disarmed his opponent. Weaponless, the larger foe, a boy with a face like a pug, bowed his head and pulled off his helmet. He walked off the mat looking embarrassed.

"He's good," said Casey, eyeing the two fighters critically. "Interesting. You don't usually see kendo in American schools."

"Kendo?" asked Monson, turning his attention to Casey. "What's that?" The term sounded vaguely familiar; he wondered where he had heard it.

"Japanese fencing." Casey peered past Monson towards the shorter fighter. "Kendo, or competitive fencing, is popular in Japanese schools, but most private schools in the States only do rapier fencing. I wonder who he is. Japanese sword fighting in the style of the *Kodachi* is really rare—"

Casey stopped as if something suddenly occurred to him. "You don't know what kendo is? How can that be? Don't you have a *bokken*?"

Monson did not have any idea what Casey was talking about. He racked his brain and came to a realization. "Oh, is that what that shiny stick is? I wondered what it was called. So it's like for fencing, right?"

"Are you messing with me? You must fence. You move like a fencer."

"Why do you say that?"

"Grey, you remember how we met, right?"

"Of course, but what does that have to do with fencing?"

"I'm a martial arts student," said Casey, smiling. "And I took up rapier fencing in elementary school and not long after that, kendo. After a while, you can just tell the people that have trained. I would have bet Arthur's weight in gold you were a fencer. The way you blocked his attack was perfect. You aren't just pulling my leg, are you? You really haven't fenced before?"

Monson struggled to answer Casey's question. Fencing. He really liked the sound of that. The mere thought made his fingers suddenly tense, but he could not remember ever fencing, and it wasn't something that struck a chord within him. They were quickly coming to the topic that Monson wanted to avoid. He thought a diversionary tactic was probably his best bet.

"So you can tell things about fighters just by observing them?" he asked casually. "What can you tell me about our vertically challenged friend over there?"

Monson pointed at the boy, who was furiously fighting a new opponent.

If Casey was aware of Monson's redirection, he did not let it show. "First a little background. The *kodachi* is a smaller blade than the *katana*, the Japanese long sword—that's made for defense. The fighting style developed for the kodachi is augmented by an aggressive hand-to-hand combat, usually kempo or some kind of jujutsu. This one, however..." He paused for a moment as he watched. "This guy doesn't seem to exhibit any of that type of tactic or style."

Casey's eyes narrowed as if he were considering something.

"Well, of course he doesn't." He sounded like he was scolding himself. "This isn't an actual battle; it's a match. He would be disqualified if he struck him with his hands. Then again, they aren't using *shinai*."

"What's a *shinai*?"

Casey brought his hands up, stretching them as he watched the fighter. He looked back at Monson.

"A *shinai* is a bamboo sword that's used in official kendo matches. They don't use *bokken*; they're too dangerous. You can break some bones or even kill someone if you aren't careful."

"Yeah," agreed Monson, returning his attention to the match. "Now that you mention it, this doesn't really look like a match, but actual combat. Not that I would really know the difference."

"Totally," Casey nodded in agreement. "They don't even have a referee. I think I'm going to talk to him. I want to know where he trained."

"Why bother?" asked Monson, who could not think of anything less practical.

Casey answered, "How could I not want to know? I mean how cool is that, seriously?"

Monson chuckled. He had a point. "Casey, what kind of martial art do you do?"

Casey's eyes lit up. "You know, that's a very interesting question. Honestly, I have no idea what it's called."

Monson raised an eyebrow in his signature gesture. "That's weird. How can you study something you don't even know the name of? Who taught you?"

"It's a family thing," commented Casey. "My dad taught me when I was very young, then my uncle took over."

"Why'd he do that?"

Casey looked uncomfortable. Apparently, Monson wasn't the only one who had things he didn't want to discuss.

"Why wouldn't your uncle tell you the name of your art? That seems weird to me."

"Yeah," said Casey matter-of-factly. "It has something to do with mastery. I dunno, I wasn't really paying attention."

"So you don't know anything about its origins?" inquired Monson, now genuinely interested.

"I didn't say that."

"Well?"

"I think it's from somewhere in China, or Asia at least."

"Wow," Monson said, laughing. "Brilliant, Holmes, brilliant. A martial art coming from Asia! Your powers of deduction are outstanding."

Casey glared at him before stalking towards the opposite side of the mat.

"Where ya going?" asked Monson, moving after him. "Come on, it was just a joke."

"You're funny. It's totally not like that. I just don't want to be over-heard, and it's kind of a long story."

They sat down on a corner of the mat away from the group still watching the fencers. Reclined in a comfortable position, Monson gave Casey the go-ahead. Casey was not paying attention, however, but was looking directly over Monson's shoulder.

"What?" Monson turned to see what Casey was looking at. Artorius was standing with the same group of girls a short distance away.

"He's never going to learn," said Casey, shaking his head and chuckling slightly. "I don't know how many times I'm going to have to say this before we need an intervention: We need to find that boy a lady."

"Poor Artorius," said Monson, smiling. He was proud he didn't laugh.

"Anyway." He returned his attention to Casey. "On with your story and make it snappy. I still need to check in with Coach Able."

"OK, OK, I get it." Casey settled back, looking thoughtful. His expression changed, becoming much more serious. "I think I came to the Asian conclusion when I was about ten." His eyes screwed up in concentration. "The first and most obvious reason was all the references to life energies."

"Life energies?"

Casey smiled. He looked like he was about to start laughing. "Has anyone ever told you that you do that a lot?"

"Do what a lot?"

"That. Answer everything with a question!"

"I do not."

"Sure you don't."

Before Monson could summon a retort, however, Casey continued. "We were talking about life energies. *Chi, ki, chakra, prana*: Different cultures have different names for them."

"So, *chakra* or *chi*?" asked Monson. This time Casey cocked an eyebrow, copying Monson's move. Monson grimaced. "I did it again, didn't I?"

"Yeah."

Monson scowled. "OK, tell me about *chakra*."

The subject was long and drawn out, and Monson did not understand everything that Casey said, but thought he had managed to catch the main points.

"So, let me get this straight," said Monson. "Through meditation and training, you can focus the life energies in your body and use them to fight?"

"Yeah, well, it's a bit more complicated than that, but you're basically right."

"No way."

"Seriously, I use it all the time in training."

"You're so full of it."

"I'll prove it." Casey stood up. "Come here."

He guided Monson to the middle of another large wrestling mat a little farther away from the other students.

"Before we start, do you think you could help me warm up a bit?"

asked Casey. "This takes some time, and it's dangerous if you use it without preparing yourself."

He paused.

"And...I have a little theory I would like to try out."

"Sure," said Monson, who was still skeptical. "What can I do to help?"

"You can defend yourself."

"I'm sorry?"

Casey leaped at Monson, attacking with amazing speed. A low kick struck him mid-thigh, but to Monson's amazement, his body reacted seemingly on its own, actually stepping into the blow and diminishing much of the force. Casey responded, and aiming for Monson's face, he threw a monstrous cross-body blow a split second after his low kick. Monson deflected this with a smooth movement of the wrist, causing the punch to miss its mark and pass harmlessly to the side. The boys held the position, giving Monson time to marvel at his actions. Casey smiled.

"You really are interesting, Grey. All right. Let's try this."

He stepped back and assumed a stance, body leaning forward, fists up and in front of him. Monson realized this was a more aggressive fighting stance—fist and elbow-oriented.

He paused. Where did that come from? How the heck would he know what kind of stance this was?

Casey did not give him time to figure this out, but Monson's instincts were correct. Quick, powerful strikes with closed and open fists, augmented with various elbow strikes, poured down on him. Monson kept his hands close to his body, using small circular movements to block the attacks. He was quite successful and matched Casey blow for blow.

More than once, however, Casey's attack patterns changed, and Monson began to understand the flow of his style. It started with the base form, or starting position of his body; when he changed his starting form, he changed his entire attack style. In the course of their short bout, Monson counted five different forms, all of which were completely different in power, speed, and emphasis. It was as if Casey grew up learning not one fighting style but five. It was a bit scary.

I shouldn't know this. The words echoed in Monson's mind.

Monson shouldn't, but he did. He could see the forms. He could see the change and flow of the different styles. It was a dangerous martial art, and Casey was very good at it. Monson wasn't sure what was more disconcerting: that he knew so much about fighting or that his new friend was so good at it. There was no explanation for this. None.

Monson did surprisingly well but took more than a few blows. His body seemed to ache as he went through the movements, as if his muscles were remembering something painful and persistent. Monson did connect with a shot or two. Casey's form-based style was as wild as his fencing. He had openings, plenty of them, but Monson just could not find the mindset or spirit he needed to take advantage of them. Their battle drove on for the better part of five minutes until a particularly vicious spinning back kick based on a flowing-type form centered around the legs barely missed Monson's head. Monson put his hand up.

"I think you're warmed up, Casey," he said, panting. "What are you trying to do? You're gonna kill me!"

"Hardly," said Casey. "I wasn't exactly going easy on you, and you're still standing. Are you sure you've never studied any kind of martial arts?"

"I could have been a French kitchen maid for all I know," said Monson without thinking. He clapped his hand over his mouth. Casey just stared at him, confusion on his face. He smiled keenly at Monson.

"We don't have to talk about it now, Grey, but I expect an explanation later."

Monson let out a sigh of relief. "Sure. Sometime."

Casey beamed at him, looking very pleased.

"Well, regardless, you're awfully good for not knowing anything. I think you and Jason Bourne might be related."

"Who's Jason Bourne?" inquired Monson.

"What!? Who's Jason Bourne!? Are you kidding me?"

"Wait. First, *chakra*. Focus."

"Oh yeah," said Casey, grinning. "I almost forgot. I think I'm ready." He paused. "But we are so watching that movie."

Casey led Monson to the middle of the mat and showed him a defensive stance. Apparently, you could easily get hurt with this...exercise. Then, stepping away, Casey started to shake the different parts of his body vigorously.

"I want to make sure that everything is loose," he said in answer to Monson's inquiring stare. "Don't want to pull a hammy."

Monson decided not to comment.

Casey finally took a position not far from where Monson was standing. He settled into a stationary stance and, closing his eyes, started to breathe deeply and slowly. He looked rather serene.

"This may hurt a little bit," he whispered. He raised his right hand, open-fisted, rested it on the palm of his left, and placed them both firmly in front of his body. Monson watched, intrigued but still a little skeptical. Events continued in this fashion until...until something changed. It was hard to describe this change. It was slight and unobtrusive, but it was almost palpable. Something about the atmosphere surrounding his friend was different. He could feel an energy emerging and becoming stronger. This change was not all that Monson had to worry about; it also felt like someone was watching them, and with a rather intense focus. The hairs on the back of Monson's neck stood up as he spoke calming words aloud to himself. He chided himself. He was being paranoid. He needed to calm down.

"Hey, Casey," said Monson, his attention splintered between his friend and his search for the source of his uneasiness. "Don't you think you should..."

Monson never finished his sentence, as the sight he was now witnessing left him speechless.

ABOUT THE AUTHOR

A native of Washington State, Collin grew up NOT liking reading stories or school in general. Girls, sports, and working held much more appeal for the young Collin. He graduated from Moses Lake High School despite lack of regular attendance then journeyed forth towards Boise State in Idaho where he received a B.A. in Social Science. His dream was to practice law with his father and brother; a dream that he pursued vigorously in his undergraduate education. Little did he know that his father would leave the practice of law and his brother would make plans to head to Costa Rica. While these career developments were unexpected, even more unexpected was Collin's growing interest in writing and story telling. After reading several stories (averaging a book a week for almost a whole year), he developed a story idea and started to write.

Podcast novels, self publishing, eBooks and writing in general were much like his move to SOUTH DAKOTA (Yes, I said South Dakota); random and totally unexpected. Collin spent a year writing a story with a Roman/Greek Gods --dragon/elves/drawfs theme then came to a real and terrible realization: Fantasy fans are brutal. Absolutely brutal! If they like you, man they REALLY like you. If they don>t...well let>s not talk about that. From that moment, Collin spent many hours reworking his first novel, The House of Grey into a story that Fantasy fans (and everyone else hopefully) will enjoy, gleaning ideas from many independent literary sources from Indian folklore to Japanese anime and taking inspiration from some of the greats like Rick Riordan, J. K. Rowling Mark Frost, Joseph Lallo, Brian Rathbone, Scott Sigler, MR Mathias, Jeff Wheeler and Nathan Lowell.

After graduating from the University of South Dakota Law School, Collin, his smoldering wife, and two beautiful daughters moved down the street from his Producer and co-author Chris Snelgrove in good ol' Colorado. Collin passed the Bar and is currently working as an attorney and vigorously writing fantastical stories for his fans.

Collin is current working on three different series - The House of Grey, Harmonics, and the third series called Daniel Knight (the Never World Series)- this story will include an alternative timeline where magic exists in the world and military power is represented by powerful "relics" from religious mythology including Zeus' master lightening bolt, Excalibur, the kusanagi and the other Imperial Regalia from Japan and much much more.

www.ingramcontent.com/pod-product-compliance
Lightning Source LLC
Chambersburg PA
CBHW050347030726
47503CB00008B/2662